'You and I need to talk, Jemma.'

'In that case, you'd better come into the kitchen. You can tell me what you have to say while I get you a cold drink.'

'I don't want a cold drink, Jemma. What I *want* is an explanation as to why you told me you were married when we met on the island a year ago. And I want you, of course...but not necessarily in that order,' Luke said softly.

Jemma responded angrily, 'Not in any order! I don't owe you an explanation; in fact, I don't even owe you the time of day, given that you're dating my stepsister.'

'Then asking you to marry me is out of the question, I take it?' Luke asked, progressing straight to Plan B with a hint of amusement in his tone.

'I wouldn't marry you if you were the last man on earth!' Jemma vowed.

'You say that now, Jemma, but you may not have a choice...'

THE GREEK TYCOONS

**They're the men who have everything—
except brides…**

Wealth, power, charm—what else could a
heart-stoppingly handsome tycoon need?

In THE GREEK TYCOONS mini-series you have
already been introduced to some gorgeous Greek
multimillionaires who are in need of wives.

Now it's the turn of favourite Modern Romance™ author
Jacqueline Baird, with her attention-grabbing romance

BOUGHT BY THE GREEK TYCOON

Luke Devetzi has met his match in Jemma Barnes, and
he's decided he *has* to have her…*whatever* that takes!

BOUGHT BY THE GREEK TYCOON

BY
JACQUELINE BAIRD

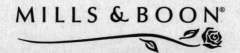

MILLS & BOON®

First published in Great Britain 2005
Paperback Edition 2006
Harlequin Mills & Boon Limited,
Eton House, 18-24 Paradise Road, Richmond, Surrey TW9 1SR

© Jacqueline Baird 2005

ISBN 0 263 84777 2

Set in Times Roman 10½ on 12 pt.
01-0106-53824

Printed and bound in Spain
by Litografia Rosés, S.A., Barcelona

CHAPTER ONE

JEMMA BARNES, pencil in hand, doodled in the notebook in front of her on the table, paying little attention to the conversation going on around her. Her father, MD of the company Vanity Flair, had insisted that she attend this board meeting now that she was heir to her late Aunt Mary's estate, and therefore now one of the principal shareholders in the company. She had no idea why he wanted her there—stock flotations and the like were a foreign language to her. In fact, she had enough trouble coping with the monetary side of her own business—as Liz, her best friend and partner in the florist shop they jointly owned in Chelsea, would readily confirm!

'Jemma?' The strident tones of her father's voice cut through her reverie. 'Do you agree?'

Lifting her head, she realised the dozen or so people around the table were all staring at her. Her amber eyes clashed with the twinkling brown ones of the man opposite—a Mr Devetzi from Greece. Her father had introduced Jemma to him earlier and she rather liked the old man. Apparently he had once met her aunt Mary at her holiday home on the island of Zante—the same place that Jemma had spent her last holiday with her aunt. It wasn't a holiday she liked to recall for a variety of reasons—one being that her aunt had died a few months later.

Now a hint of a smile played around the old man's mouth, and she knew he'd realised from her panicked expression that she had no idea of the question. His smile broadened reassuringly, and with a wink and a nod of his white head he gave her the answer.

'Yes, of course, Father,' Jemma agreed, and the meeting ended.

'Why on earth didn't you get in touch with me?' Luke Devetzi demanded forcibly in Greek, and stared down at his grandfather, lounging back on the sofa with one heavily bandaged ankle propped up on a footstool. 'You know I would have come the minute you called.' He raked frustrated fingers through his dark hair. 'And what are you doing in London anyway? After your last heart scare I seem to recall your doctor forbidding you to travel.'

'Business,' Theo Devetzi declared bluntly.

'But you retired from the fish business years ago,' Luke reminded him.

'Not *that* business. As a matter of fact I did call you six days ago, but I was informed by some woman in your New York office that you had already left for a long weekend in the Hamptons and were not to be disturbed unless it was a dire emergency.' The old man arched one sardonic eyebrow. 'As it was only a courtesy call, to tell you I was going to use your London apartment for a few days, I saw no reason to bother you.'

Luke stifled a grimace, but he had no defence; he had left just such instructions, and he felt guilty as hell. His grandparents had turned their lives upside down thirty-eight years ago when Anna, their only daughter, had got pregnant by a yachtsman visiting the Greek island where they lived. Unwilling to subject Anna and her unborn child to the censure of the small community, they had relocated to Athens, where no one knew them. Then, when Anna had died in childbirth, they had been left to bring Luke up on their own.

Luke had never known who his biological father was until after he'd graduated from university at the age of twenty-one, with a degree in Business Studies. He had refused to follow his grandfather into the wholesale fish business, instead signing up as assistant purser on a luxury cruise liner. In a fit of temper Theo had declared he was just like his feckless French father—a so-called aristocrat who spent his life sailing around in his yacht seducing young girls. In the ensuing argument Luke had discovered his grandfather had known his father's name all along.

Luke had stormed out and gone to find his father. He had discovered the man living on a large estate in France—with his wife and two sons both older than Luke. When Luke had confronted him he had sneered and disowned him with the words, 'I have had dozens of women in my life, and even if I had been single at the time I would never have married your Greek peasant of a mother.' Then, with the help of his two equally obnoxious sons, he'd had Luke thrown off his land.

Luke had gone ahead and joined the cruise liner. There he had struck up a friendship with an elderly New York banker, who had enlisted Luke's aid in reading the stock market. When the ship had docked in New York, impressed by Luke's natural ability to spot a winner, the same man had offered Luke a job with his firm. Luke had become the proverbial whiz kid, and four years later had started his own investment banking company—Devetzi International.

The circumstances of his birth no longer bothered Luke, and hadn't done for years. He viewed his grandfather's set features now with a mixture of frustration and love. 'Nothing you do or want can ever be too much trouble for me, Theo. You only have to ask and it will be given. You must know that.'

Theo was getting old. His heavily lined face showed the signs of his seventy-seven years, and yet his deep brown eyes still held the determination that had seen him build up a business with his best friend Milo. Luke owed his life to this man.. as far as he was concerned Theo was the only family he had.

'Humph. Fine words, Lycurgus, but they cut no ice with me.'

Luke stiffened. He knew the old man was always either angry or after something when he used Luke's full name—chosen for him by his grandmother because it meant wolf-hunter, and his silver-grey eyes had reminded her of a wolf.

'What I *wanted* was to see you married with children, to see the continuation of our bloodline. But given your apparent aversion to marriage and your choice in women I have almost given up hope.' Lifting a magazine from the coffee table, he waved it at Luke. 'Just look at your latest woman—probably the one you have spent the last few days with.' He flicked to the centre page. 'Davina Lovejoy is about as likely to make a good wife and mother as fly,' he snorted.

Theo was right—Luke had been dating Davina for the last few weeks and had spent a long weekend with the lady in question. He could tell his grandfather that he had no intention of marrying the lady anyway.. but, dammit, why should he? He didn't exactly appreciate Theo interfering in his sex life. And, as for marriage, Luke had little trust in women for the long term. In his experience he had found the married ones just as eager to get into his bed as the single women he met, if not more so—not that he was at all interested in getting involved with married women. The only exception to that particular rule still nagged his conscience to this day…

Belatedly he tuned back in to Theo's rapid-fire Greek.
'...and I thought you had more taste, but obviously I
was wrong. Have you read this?' Theo waved the magazine again. 'She had a nose job at nineteen! That I can
understand, and even the breast enhancement I could tolerate, but this last thing... Well, I have never heard of
anything like it in my life! A false bottom! You might as
well take a plastic doll to your bed,' he exclaimed.

'*What?* Let me see that,' Luke snapped, and took the
magazine from Theo's hand. A quick glance told him his
grandfather was right. A photograph of Davina and himself leaving a restaurant—a month earlier, if he wasn't
mistaken—followed by an article all about Davina, her
physical enhancements, and the new man in her life.

A vitriolic Greek curse escaped him, and he flung the
magazine back on the table in disgust.

'My sentiments exactly,' Theo agreed, with the
slightest of smiles lightening his leathered face.

Luke ran his hand through his dark hair again. 'I never
even realised,' he muttered. And, as he considered himself
something of a connoisseur of women, that was some admission!

Sinking down onto the sofa beside Theo, he gave the
old man a wry smile. 'I met Davina because she's an
interior designer, and my PA in New York hired her to
redecorate my apartment in the city. Propinquity did the
rest.' He didn't add that it had only been when showing
the woman around his apartment it had suddenly struck
him he had not bedded a woman in over a year and it was
time he did something about it. 'But if it gives you any
satisfaction, Theo, I have no intention of marrying her.'

When the apartment was finished, in a couple of weeks,
so would be his involvement with Davina. Beautiful and
intelligent though she was, this last weekend had not been

the roaring success he had hoped for. Davina was a very experienced lover, and the sex had been good, but for some reason it had left him feeling oddly unsatisfied.

'Good! In that case you can do me a favour,' Theo stated. 'Since your grandmother's death I've been making a few discreet enquiries about buying back my family home on Zante. I sold it to the local butcher when we moved from the island to Athens, but the house and the cove had been in my family for generations. I want it back,' he declared emphatically. 'I was conceived on that beach, I courted your grandmother there, and your mother was conceived on the same beach. It has a thousand happy memories for me, and when you get to my age that is about all you have left.'

Theo sighed deeply, then went on, 'I did some digging and discovered the butcher died eight years later, and his family sold it for cash to a nameless businessman from Athens. According to gossip, he then gifted it to his mistress—an Englishwoman called Mary James; a botanist from London. I caught up with her on the island one time. She was a lovely lady, and she told me about her work and the company she had founded with her sister called Vanity Flair, producing a line of homeopathic, anti-allergenic make-up. Later, her sister married the company accountant, one David Sutherland, and he was instrumental in expanding the business into retail outlets all over Europe.

'But when I asked her if she would sell me the house on Zante she flatly refused, and closed up like a clam. So when I heard the company was to be floated on AIM— the alternative investment market in London—with the intention of raising money to fund expansion into America, I bought a block of shares on the off-chance that at some point they might give me some leverage in trying to persuade Miss James into selling my family home back to me.'

Luke frowned. Most of the companies floated on AIM were high-risk businesses. 'Take my advice—sell up and get out now. As for your old home—forget it. Anyway, I thought you liked living in the house I had built for us all? You have never complained.'

'No, but, beautiful as it is, since your grandmother died I find it a bit lonely—you're rarely there.'

'A good point,' Luke conceded. The fact that he'd had no idea Theo was interested in buying back the property on Zante shamed him, and revealed just how little real attention he had given his grandfather in the past few years, how much he had taken him for granted. 'I promise I will try to get home more often, Theo. But it doesn't alter the fact that Zante is a very popular tourist destination now. It's nothing like when you lived there—you'd hate it.' Luke knew because he had berthed his yacht for one night on the island last summer, and, beautiful though the scenery still was, he had departed quickly the next morning.

'No, you're wrong. At last I can see a way to recover what was once mine.' Theo's eyes sparkled with more excitement than Luke had seen in a long time. 'I discovered that Mary James died some months ago, and I immediately started to buy up more stock.' Theo held up a veined hand. 'And before you say it, I know the stock has been falling recently—but that was to my advantage because I got it cheap.'

If the company went down the tubes it wouldn't be cheap, but Luke shook his head and kept his mouth shut, not wanting to argue further with Theo.

'I received a call last week to attend a special board meeting of Vanity Flair, as one of the larger stockholders.

I went to the meeting on Friday, and I had a drink with Sutherland afterwards. The only reason I've stayed on here the last few days was because he's invited me to dinner at his house this evening, and also to his daughter's birthday party this coming weekend.'

'That's very interesting, but it doesn't explain how you sprained your ankle, nor that if Milo hadn't contacted me in New York last night I would have known nothing about it.'

'Yes, you would. Because I was going to call you myself as soon as I got back from the hospital but Milo pre-empted me. Incidentally, I sprained my ankle yesterday, tripping down the steps of this damn fool sunken living room of yours.' He looked disdainfully around the plush curving black hide seating arrangement in the obviously bachelor penthouse.

'Well, at least you had the sense to bring Milo with you,' Luke murmured. 'This is a service apartment, and I hate to think what might have happened if you'd been on your own.'

'Naturally he came with me,' Theo said. 'Milo is just as keen as I am to see me get my family home back. Zante is where he and I first met and became friends. He used to stay with your grandmother and I whenever his fishing boat came into the harbour. I always thought he had a soft spot for your mother, but it wasn't to be...'

Luke almost groaned, wishing Theo would get to the point, but he knew from experience that there was no way to hurry him. 'So, how are you going to get it back, then?' he enquired.

'I'm not. You are,' Theo declared with a broad grin. 'I met Sutherland's daughter at the board meeting. She's a delightful woman who knows nothing at all about the family business—though she does run her own. We had an interesting conversation, and I discovered she was attending the meeting only because her father had told her to. She inherited everything from her aunt—shares in the company and, more importantly, the property on Zante.'

'Thank heaven for that.' Luke rose and crossed to the drinks trolley, poured a slug of whisky into a glass and added a generous splash of iced water. 'So the daughter is selling it and you want me to pay for it, right? No problem…' Lifting the glass to his mouth, he took a refreshing drink, watching the old man with tender eyes.

'No, I'd just got around to asking her if she would sell the villa, and she'd just told me she didn't think she could, when the meeting was called to order. I don't need your money, but I do need you to go to the dinner party tonight in my place. Use some of that skill you have at charming the ladies on the daughter. Show her a good time—wine and dine her for the rest of the week and soften her up a bit. Then, when I attend her birthday party on Saturday night, I can appeal to her finer feelings and explain to her that it is an old man's wish to own the home of his ancestors and pass it on to his grandson. When I ask her again to sell me the property, she will be ready to say yes to anything she thinks you want.'

'You want me to seduce her, you mean?' Luke met Theo's intent gaze and lifted one eyebrow in mocking cynicism. 'You do surprise me, considering you have spent years complaining about my womanising ways. Shame on you, Theo!'

'You don't need go that far—not that it would be any hardship, I'm sure, for she is a very lovely lady.' Theo grinned. 'If I was forty years younger, I'd be there myself.'

Luke laughed. 'You're incorrigible, old man, but okay. You arrange with Sutherland for me to dine in your place tonight, and I will do my level best to charm the woman. In the meantime, I need to shower and dress.' Draining his drink, he added, 'What is the woman's name?'

Theo was already reaching for the telephone to call Sutherland. 'J something…Jem…or Jan, I think,' his grandfather said, dialling a number.

Rolling his shoulders to relieve the ache in his back from long hours of travel and tension, Luke headed for his bedroom wondering just what he had let himself in for, hoping this Jan woman would turn out to be halfway presentable.

It was after midnight when Luke finally returned to his apartment..tired, but with a self-satisfied smile on his darkly handsome face.

'So what happened? Did you meet her? Did you like her? And, more importantly, did she like you?' Theo demanded as soon as he walked in the door.

'Yes to all three.' Luke grinned. 'But you shouldn't have waited up.'

'Never mind that…just tell me what happened.'

Luke collapsed on the sofa and loosened his tie and shirt collar. 'I met Sutherland and he introduced me to his daughter Jan, and by an amazing coincidence I knew her.'

'You *knew* her? Are you sure?'

'Believe me, old man, I know her. I met her in New York years ago. She was working as a model then, and I dated her a few times. So you have absolutely nothing to worry about; the deal is virtually in the bag, I promise you. Jan was delighted to see me, and was all over me like a rash. I'm taking her out to dinner tomorrow night, and by the party on Saturday she will be desperate to gobble me whole.' Rising to his feet, Luke added, 'Now, if you don't mind, I'm going to bed—and I suggest you do the same.'

'Phone, Jemma—it's your stepmother,' Liz yelled.

Busy in the workshop, planting a hanging basket with summer annuals, Jemma didn't appreciate the interruption. Sighing, she put down her tools, pulled off her protective gloves and picked up the extension on the workbench.

'Yes, Leanne?' Jemma only half listened to her stepmother for the next few minutes. Her own mother had died when she was twelve, after a long illness, and her father had married his secretary six months later—a single mother with a sixteen-year-old daughter, Janine, who had already left school and started a career as a model.

At the time Jemma had been attending boarding school, so the two girls had not been very close—more friends than family—but her father had officially adopted Janine, so they all shared the same surname.

'You do understand, Jemma?'

'Yes, perfectly.' Jemma finally got a chance to speak. 'I've ordered all the flowers you requested, and I'll be there early on Saturday to decorate the house for Jan's birthday party.' Jemma put the phone down and glanced at Liz. 'You're sure you don't mind managing with just young Patty on Saturday afternoon? We could close the shop and you could come with me?'

'No, thanks,' Liz replied. 'You know I can only take the beautiful Janine in very small doses. What birthday is it this time—her twenty-eighth for the fourth year running?'

'Don't be catty! But you're right—although I've been sworn to secrecy. Hey, apparently Jan met an old boyfriend at the dinner party last night.'

'The same dinner party you ducked out of, pleading a headache yet again?' Liz mocked.

'Yes—well, apparently he is still a bachelor and incredibly wealthy. Jan wants to hook him, so there's to be absolutely no mention of her real age.'

'Why doesn't that surprise me?' Liz chuckled, a wicked glint in her dark eyes.

'Naughty!' Jemma smiled.

'I only wish *you* would be naughty once in a while.' Liz sighed. 'It's time you got out and enjoyed yourself again.'

'Well, I am going to the party on Saturday,' Jemma said, walking across to the centre counter and taking the order book from Liz's hand. 'And it's time you went for lunch. Patty's due back any minute, and Ray won't be long.' Patty was a trainee and Ray was a qualified florist, but he spent most of his time as their delivery driver.

'Okay, I'm going. But I mean it, Jemma. Alan has been dead two years now, and, much as you loved him, it is time you started dating again—or at least considered the possibility, instead of freezing out every handsome man who so much as smiles at you. Haven't you heard? Apart from being no fun, total celibacy is bad for one's health.'

To Jemma's undying shame, she had *not* been totally celibate in the last two years—she had made one enormous mistake, which she had vowed never to repeat, but she didn't have the nerve to tell her best friend the truth. Instead Jemma threw a damp florist's sponge at her. 'Go to lunch!'

She watched a laughing Liz duck out of the door and sighed, flicking through the order book without actually reading it. She had already met and married her soul mate, and then she had lost him.

It had all started when Jemma had begun to spend most of her free time with Aunt Mary, after the death of her mother. Her father had sold the family home with its large garden and bought an impressive townhouse for his new wife. But Jemma loved gardening, and her aunt had allowed her a free hand in her garden. As a lecturer at Imperial College London, her Aunt Mary and her work as a botanist had fascinated Jemma, but her aunt's young research assistant, Alan Barnes, had fascinated her more. She'd developed an enormous crush on him, and he had become her best friend and confidante.

Later, when she'd left school at eighteen, she'd known she didn't have the academic brain to follow in her aunt's footsteps. But what she did have was an artistic flair with plants, and she had enrolled on a two-year course in floristry at a local college—which was where she'd met Liz. Jemma's relationship with Alan had grown into a deep, abiding love, and it had been with his encouragement that Jemma and Liz had opened their shop together. Life had been great, and it had only got better when, at the age of twenty-two, Jemma had married Alan Barnes in a fairytale wedding.

Tragically, they had only been married for a brief four years when Alan had been killed in a gliding accident—a sport both he and Jemma had enjoyed. She still felt guilty that she had not been with him on the fatal day; instead she had stayed in London to complete a large order to decorate the old Assembly Rooms for a charity gala that evening.

Thinking about Alan now still squeezed her heart with sadness, but, thanks to Liz's unfailing support over the past two years, she had at least got over crying at the thought of him and could now face the world, as content as she would ever be.

The wind chimes over the door rang, and Jemma glanced up as a customer walked in. She banished her memories to the back of her mind and smiled. 'Can I help you?'

Luke glanced down at the elegant blonde who had attached herself to his arm the moment the maid had shown him and Theo into the drawing room of the large Georgian mansion in Connaught Square that was the Sutherland home. 'Happy birthday, Jan.' He had given her a present last night: nothing too personal—a Prada handbag. 'And my grandfather I think you know—'

She didn't let him finish. 'Oh, yes, I know. How terrible…' She flashed a smile in Theo's direction. 'I was so sorry to hear you'd hurt your ankle. But I can't deny I was delighted Luke came to dinner in your place.' Then, turning her eyes up to Luke, she gushed, 'It was fate we met again. Isn't that right, darling?' And she tilted her head back for his kiss.

'Probably,' Luke murmured, smiling down at his companion. Jan was a sophisticated lady who knew the score; he had met her type a thousand times and it was no hardship to dip his head and brush his lips briefly against her scarlet mouth. Though it did surprise him that Theo found her attractive; he wouldn't have thought a six-foot-tall, rake-thin model would be his grandfather's type at all.

The noise hit Jemma first as she descended the staircase. She cast a professional eye over the flower display on the hall table and, satisfied, reluctantly turned towards the source of the noise. She had very rarely attended large parties since Alan's death, but this was one she could not avoid.

Straightening her shoulders, she walked into the

crowded drawing room and glanced around, her gaze alighting on the birthday girl. Jan was gazing up at a man who had his back to Jemma. Her perfectly made-up face was lifted to his, anticipating a kiss, and he duly obliged. Well over six foot tall, with broad shoulders and black hair, he looked impressive even from the back—and he was a perfect foil for Jan's model height and sleek blonde hair.

They made a striking couple, Jemma thought idly, and let her gaze drift away—only to suddenly focus on an old man standing on his own and watching the embracing couple. He was leaning heavily on a silver-topped cane and had an expression of total bewilderment on his weathered face—a face she instantly recognised. He looked as out of place as Jemma felt, and swiftly she moved towards him.

'Mr Devetzi.' She smiled at her saviour from the board meeting. 'It's lovely to see you again.' She offered her hand and he gratefully grasped it.

'It is my privilege,' he replied, and with old-world courtesy raised her hand and kissed it. 'Please call me Theo.'

'Theo it is, you old charmer.' Jemma laughed.

Luke felt Theo tug frantically on the sleeve of his jacket at exactly the same moment as he recognised the soft feminine voice. He turned slowly and saw the woman holding his grandfather's hand and smiling into his eyes, flirting with him… He tensed, every muscle in his body locking in shock and outrage. He knew her in the most intimate way possible; she had haunted his dreams for the past year, and he despised her for her lack of morals even as his body still ached for her. But, before he could formulate a suitably cutting greeting, Jan's grip on his other arm tightened and she spoke to the woman.

'Jemma, darling, meet Luke—the wonderful man I was telling you about.'

Luke heard Jan's voice, but only registered the name. *Jemma.* So what had happened to *Mimie*? he thought cynically. Obviously it was a pseudonym she used when cheating on her husband! But, however unfaithful she was, it didn't alter the fact that she looked even more incredible than he remembered.

The first and only time he had seen her until this party had been a year ago, when he and a group of his friends had taken a cruise around the Greek islands in his yacht for a couple of weeks—something he did every summer. It had been the birthday of one of the female guests, and they had partied on board and then gone ashore to the island of Zante to eat.

It had been when he'd slipped out of the restaurant full of tourists to stroll along the harbour and clear his head a little from the smoke and noise that he had noticed her. She had been sitting at a table outside a local harbour bar, sipping a glass of red wine, and she'd looked as if she had just stepped out of a Rossetti painting. She'd worn no make-up, yet she'd been stunningly beautiful. Her face was fine-boned, with high cheekbones and a short, straight nose over a perfectly formed mouth; her lips were full and a natural pink. Her hair was tucked behind her delicate ears to fall long and straight down her back, and was a rich chestnut gilded with reds and golds that reminded him of the changing leaves in autumn.

As he had watched a couple of locals had walked from the bar and bumped into her table, sending her glass and a half-empty carafe of red wine all over her. She had leapt to her feet, and Luke had leapt to her rescue.

She had willingly accepted his offer to accompany him to his yacht to clean the stains from the brief white top and shorts she'd worn. The sex that had followed was the best he had ever had, and a certain part of his anatomy rose instantly along with his anger as he recalled what had happened afterwards. Avoiding his gaze, she had jumped off the bed and said she needed the bathroom. Picking up her clothes and purse, she had dashed into the shower room.

When she had returned from the bathroom, fully dressed, she'd been pushing a ring onto her wedding finger. Luke had rolled off the bed, reluctant to accept the evidence of his own eyes. 'You're engaged,' he'd said.

And had been met with, 'No..married. And this was a huge mistake.'

Luke had dated dozens of women, and slept with quite a few, but he never, ever got involved with married women. Furious with himself as much as her, he had said scathingly, 'Not on my part, honey. You were hot, but you'd better trot along now. My guests will be back any minute, and I'd rather they didn't see you—especially one woman in particular.'

She had looked at him, her eyes widening in horror as she'd realised what he had implied. Then she'd spun on her heel and left without a word, leaving him standing there naked, furious and disgusted with them both. He hadn't had a one-night stand since he was a teenager, and had made it a rule to date a woman at least three times before going any further. But that night he had broken his own rule—and with a married woman too...

Looking at her now, she appeared so composed, so elegant, it was hard to believe she was the passionate woman who had shared his bed. Her long hair was swept up in an intricate twist on top of her head, revealing the perfection of her features and the swan-like curve of her neck. It was enhanced by the platinum chain she wore, from which a finely tooled locket with a diamond set in the centre was suspended.

She was wearing a simple but superbly designed black dress, with minimal sleeves and a low square neckline that revealed the creamy curve of her high, firm breasts. The fabric was fine and faithfully followed the line of her shapely body and the gentle swell of her hips to end an inch or so above her knees. As for her legs, they were fabulous—their length accentuated by the high-heeled sandals that revealed pink toenails. She was utter perfection from head to toe, and a vivid mental image of her naked body beneath him, her long legs locked around his waist, made Luke catch his breath. For the first time in his life he was jealous of his grandfather. *He* wanted to be the focus of her laughs, her gorgeous smile…

No, he didn't—she was *married*! Luke reminded himself forcibly.

Jemma had heard the name Luke but thought nothing of it. She smiled at Jan and glanced politely at the man at her side. Then her eyes widened in horror, the blood drained from her face, and swiftly she lowered her gaze, her heart pounding in her breast. Jan's Luke stood head and shoulders above the crowd, immaculately dressed in a black dinner suit, and with his dark good looks he exuded an aura of arrogant assurance coupled with virile masculinity that was almost impossible to ignore. But ignore him she did.

Jemma couldn't believe it—the one mistake in her whole life was standing a foot away from her! She hadn't even known his full name, and yet she had slept with him. No.. there had been no sleep involved at all. They'd had sex, illicit sex, nothing more. She'd hated herself and despised him even more, as he'd obviously been unfaithful to the girlfriend staying with him on his yacht at the time.

Her stomach churning, and with a terrific effort of will, Jemma murmured, 'How nice to meet you.' With barely a glance at Luke, she turned back to concentrate her attention on Theo.

CHAPTER TWO

IT WAS a completely new experience for Luke Devetzi, and not one he appreciated. Amber eyes had flicked coolly in his direction and then returned to Theo, and he didn't like it at all… While not thrilled to acknowledge the lovely Jemma with Jan hanging on his arm, he was not prepared to let the promiscuous little vixen get away with ignoring him.

'Hello…*Jemma*, is it?' Luke murmured provocatively.

She glanced back at him, her amber eyes shielded by the ridiculous length of her dark lashes. 'Yes. Hello.' And as quickly she looked away again.

'As we have not been *formally* introduced, allow me. Luke Devetzi.'

He was determined to make her aware of him, and deliberately he reached out a hand towards her. A frozen glance from the golden eyes, and a small hand was offered. He grasped it, feeling the softness of her skin against his palm, and was aware of an immediate stirring in his loins. He had never been so instantly aroused by a woman since the last time he had met Jemma—no, Mimie—or whatever the hell she called herself! He looked down at their clasped hands almost in shock, and then he saw the wedding ring and remembered just in time. He did not mess with married women—except this particular sexy siren hadn't told him she was married until after he had taken her to bed.

Cold with shock, Jemma heard the seductive tone of his voice, noted the masculine challenge in his gaze and

24

caught the knowing gleam of sensuality in his grey eyes. Appalled, she quickly extricated her hand from his grasp.

'Jemma Barnes,' she muttered.

Almost on cue, Jan cut in. 'Will you do me a favour, Jemma, and take care of Luke's grandfather? He had an accident a few days ago and can't walk very well,' she said with her usual insensitivity. 'We need to circulate, and David wants to discuss business with Luke later.'

Insensitive or not, Jemma could have kissed Jan for the interruption. 'No problem. It will be my pleasure.' Jan grasped Luke's arm and the couple began moving away through the crowd. Jemma heaved a shaky sigh of relief, but inside she was trembling. Talk about worst nightmares! Luke Devetzi was up there at the very top of her list.

She was amazed he was related to Theo, for Theo was small and stocky, with dark eyes, whereas Luke had to be six foot four, and his eyes were light grey, a stark contrast to his olive-skinned complexion. His eyes were the first thing she had noticed about him a year ago, when they'd met, and they were one of the reasons she had acted so completely out of character.

That he should turn up here in her father's house, as her stepsister's boyfriend, had to be the worst coincidence ever. She felt sick to her stomach and wanted to leave. She turned back to Theo, about to make some excuse, and saw he was still staring after Jan. The expression on his face was one of utter amazement. Jemma knew exactly how she felt—only she was sure it wasn't for the same reason! 'Jan is very beautiful, and she does tend to have a surprising effect on men, but I think your grandson can handle her,' she offered reassuringly. 'And they do make a nice couple.'

He made some unintelligible comment and, raising a hand to his mouth, began to cough violently.

Leaving wasn't an option just yet—the man was obviously in difficulty. 'You're not well, Theo. I think you and I should find somewhere comfortable to sit and I'll get you a glass of champagne,' Jemma suggested, taking his arm. 'Then you can tell me all about your accident—and what I voted for last Friday,' she joked weakly.

'Certainly.' He smiled back a little shakily. 'But first can you tell me who that woman with my grandson is?' Theo gestured with his silver-topped cane in their direction.

'That's my stepsister—Jan,' Jemma told him as she finally spied a vacant sofa and led him towards the far corner of the elegant drawing room. She felt him stumble. 'Are you all right?' she asked anxiously, and helped him sit down. 'You look a little pale.' She studied his lined face with worried eyes.

'Your stepsister, you say? I didn't know you had a sister.'

'Well, you hardly know me.' Jemma laughed.

'I think I need that drink,' Theo Devetzi rasped as he settled down on the sofa, and then muttered something in Greek that to Jemma sounded suspiciously like a curse.

'If you'll wait here, I'll go and get you a brandy. It will do you more good than champagne,' Jemma offered. The man was obviously still in some pain, she thought compassionately.

Meanwhile, Luke had placed a hand on Jan's back and escorted her through the crowd. He smiled, and continued to smile in all the right places, while Jan accepted effusive birthday congratulations from her friends and they made their way towards her mother and father at the far end of the room. Luke could act the perfect consort without a thought, and his thoughts were centred on the lovely Jemma.

He glanced around the room, wondering which man was her husband. He was a lucky man—or maybe not so lucky, Luke thought cynically. There had been no mistaking the sexual chemistry, the wild passion between Jemma and himself. Her poor husband was more to be pitied than envied, he concluded.

But it was time he concentrated on Jan and did what he was here to do—help his grandfather. He glanced around the room and spotted Theo, safely seated, and briefly their eyes met. For a second Luke thought he saw panic in his grandfather's gaze, but as he watched Jemma approached and handed Theo a brandy, and the old man was all smiles.

Jemma handed the brandy glass to Theo. 'You're sure you're okay?' she queried, sitting down beside him and taking a good swallow from her own glass of champagne. She wasn't normally a drinker, but dear heaven she needed something to steady her nerves and her stomach…

'Much better,' Theo reassured her, and took a sip of brandy. 'Your sister Jan seems to know Luke well. Have you ever met him before?' he asked casually.

'No.' Jemma gritted her teeth and lied. She had no intention of letting this sweet old man know what had happened between her and Luke a year ago. 'But Jan has known him for years, I believe,' she answered. Poor Theo started coughing again. 'You sound as if you have caught a cold; are you sure you should be out so soon after your accident?'

'No, really, I'm fine,' Theo insisted, and then changed the subject by explaining to her what she had voted for at the board meeting—apparently she had agreed to another stock flotation to raise money.

'It doesn't make much difference to me,' Jemma said lightly. 'I'm mildly dyslexic with numbers, and what I know about high finance wouldn't cover my little fingernail. But I wouldn't say no to the money.' Draining her glass, she put it down on a convenient table, as did Theo.

'Well, there's a simple answer to that.' Theo took his opportunity swiftly. 'You could sell me your aunt's villa on Zante. It used to be my family home years ago, you know. Call me sentimental, but I'd rather like it back. I'm willing to give you well above the market value for it if you agree.'

'It's a nice thought, and I really would if I could, but I can't sell it to you.' Jemma saw Theo's puzzlement and explained. 'Aunt Mary left it in trust for me, and for my children, and for my children's children, *ad infinitum*— all tied up legally.'

'I see.' The old man's dark eyes narrowed thoughtfully. 'Have you ever considered applying to have the trust broken? I believe it is possible.'

'Maybe some day.' When she was too old to have children, she thought. 'But it's not something I would contemplate at the moment...' Plus, she owed it to her aunt Mary to follow her wishes, she thought with a tinge of sadness, but she saw no reason to tell Theo the whole story.

'Of course that is entirely your prerogative,' Theo said quietly, and raised his hands palms up in a gesture of defeat. 'No matter. I have lived long enough to know that one never gets everything one wants in life.' Suddenly he smiled and glanced across the room. 'Not that my grandson is often thwarted. Now, tell me honestly, what do you think of Luke?'

He is a sexual predator, skilled in the art of seduction, and he preys on the weakness of women, Jemma thought, but didn't say it. 'He seems…nice.' She lied through her teeth again. 'And I know Jan thinks very highly of him.'

At the other side of the room Luke appeared to concentrate his attention on the Sutherlands, while in his mind he ran through the report he had read this morning. His London office had done some checking over the past two days—David Sutherland was a man in trouble and trying not to show it, he thought cynically. But, smiling down at the man and his wife, he exchanged a polite greeting with the couple.

Luke already had a pretty good idea what Sutherland wanted from him. He had hinted as much on Wednesday evening once he'd realised Luke was the owner of Devetzi International. Sutherland wanted him to invest in Vanity Flair, or at the very least recommend it as a buy to his clients, in order to boost the share price and thus help Sutherland's much-vaunted expansion plans. Luke had no intention of doing either, but he had to play it cagey for the moment.

On the two occasions he had taken Jan out this week he had refrained from mentioning her inheritance to her. He had kept their relationship on a light, flirtatious level. But she had a great ability to talk about herself, and the model agency she had recently set up, which tied in with what Theo had said about her now owning her own business.

Reminded of Theo, he glanced around the room and spotted him, still sitting on the sofa, the faithless Jemma Barnes beside him. But as Luke watched the old man turned slightly, his dark eyes clashing with Luke's, and with a somewhat frantic wave of his cane he beckoned him over. What had happened now?

'Excuse me,' Luke said abruptly. 'But my grandfather

appears to need me.' And with a brief apologetic smile at Jan and her parents he moved quickly through the crowd to Theo's side.

He was met by a torrent of Greek. The gist of it being that Luke was the biggest idiot in Christendom. What was he doing hanging on to the blonde beanpole? There were two daughters and he was dating the wrong one—the step-daughter. Was he mad? *Jemma* was the one he should have been dating, and now—short of a miracle—he had blown Theo's chances of ever getting his home back.

Stunned by the news, Luke glanced at Jemma and back to Theo, feeling like a prize idiot. Then anger took over and he shot back in Greek. How the hell was he supposed to know there were *two* daughters when Theo had not even known and it had been Theo himself who'd told Luke the woman's name was Jan?

Luke's grey eyes narrowed angrily on the downbent head of the lady in question..he wasn't surprised she couldn't face him—then he glared at his grandfather. He must have been mad to let himself get involved with Theo's crazy idea in the first place. Now he'd have to extricate himself from a relationship with Jan he'd never had any enthusiasm for in the first place. And it wouldn't be easy. He began to tell Theo so in no uncertain terms.

Jemma could tell the two men were arguing, and, much as she hated the idea of facing Luke, her compassion for poor Theo overcame her fear. Rising to her feet, she cut into the tirade of Greek in a cool, well-modulated voice. 'Excuse me, Mr Devetzi, your grandfather is not very well, and shouting at him will certainly not help.'

Jemma was telling *him* off! Luke was struck dumb at the nerve of the woman.

'He's had an accident, in case you've forgotten, and he should really be at home resting.'

'I was *not* shouting.' Luke finally found his voice. 'We Greeks are as passionate in conversation as we are in everything,' he said pointedly, none too subtly reminding her of the passion they had shared. 'And I know very well what Theo needs.' He shot a lethal glance at Theo to see the man was smiling; he was enjoying this, damn him! Luke was determined Theo wasn't going to make him the villain of the evening, and neither was he taking any cheek from a married woman who quite happily slept around, he thought furiously. No matter how gorgeous she was.

'I tried to make him stay at home, but he insisted on coming to the party because he wanted to meet you again, Jemma,' Luke said. 'Apparently you made quite an impression on him at the board meeting, because he hasn't stopped talking about you. He told me you were in business, but he omitted to mention you had a partner...' He paused and deliberately looked down at her ring finger before adding, 'But then his English is not so good.' Luke offered a withering glance to his grandfather, as the old man had obviously still not realised the woman was married. 'Is your husband here? I would quite like to meet him,' he asked pointedly, his steel-grey gaze roaming insultingly over her. His question was to inform Theo of his basic mistake, but also to act as a barbed reminder to the sexy Jemma that there had been no mention of a husband while Luke had been making love to her...

Jemma could do nothing about the sudden colour that surged in her cheeks at his blatant male scrutiny and his sly dig at her married state. But, having suffered constantly as a child at the hands of her peer group because of her slight dyslexia, she wasn't prepared to stand by and let the arrogant Luke belittle his grandfather's use of the English language.

She cast Theo a sympathetic glance. 'There's nothing wrong with your English. I can understand you perfectly,' she assured him, before lifting her head to glare up at the man towering over her. 'And you should know better than to demean your grandfather's abilities in front of others,' Jemma said tautly, her glittering golden eyes clashing angrily with grey. It was as if they were the only two in the room, the tension between them a palpable force. 'And maybe if you learned to listen to your grandfather properly you wouldn't need to do it. As it happens I *do* have a partner, my best friend Liz, though I actually never told Theo I had a partner when we first met.' Implying Luke was a liar. 'And, as for my husband, he died some time ago now. Are you satisfied?'

For the second time in as many minutes Luke was stunned into silence as he thought of the opportunity he might have had with her if Theo had got his facts right. The beautiful Jemma was free and single again… He didn't really care when her husband had died; it was enough to know she was available now—except for the minor complication that he was currently dating her stepsister… Damage limitation was called for—and fast!

Straightening his shoulders, he caught the flicker of sadness in her huge amber eyes that she could not quite disguise and he felt like a heel.

'I'm so sorry, Jemma. I never meant to offend you or Theo. May I offer my deepest sympathy at the loss of your husband?'

'Thank you,' Jemma responded curtly, finally tearing her gaze away from his, and not believing him for a second. She was too shocked to say anything more. Luke Devetzi had angered her so much that she had blurted out in public that Alan was dead—something she had rarely had the strength to do before—and it scared her.

'Forgive my grandson for being so crass. I know exactly how you feel,' Theo cut in, and she was grateful for the old man's intervention. 'I have also lost my wife, but let me assure you it does get easier.' After giving her a sympathetic smile he looked back at his grandson. 'But Jemma is right, Luke, perhaps I was a bit hasty in coming out tonight.' Suddenly rising to his feet, with more agility than Jemma would have thought him capable of, he grasped Luke's arm—just as Jan appeared.

'Luke, darling, is everything all right?'

Looking from Theo to Luke and back again, Jemma had the oddest feeling some silent communication had passed between them.

Jan placed a proprietorial hand on Luke's shirtfront.

'No, my grandfather isn't feeling too well, so I am going to take him straight home. Sorry we have to leave early, but it is necessary,' Luke said smoothly.

'Oh, must you?' Jan pouted 'Surely you can stay, even if your grandfather has to leave? I'll call him a cab.'

'No, I couldn't possibly allow him to go home alone.' Luke removed Jan's hand from his chest, his tone hard, and Jemma had a feeling that Jan had just made a big mistake with this man.

'Oh, but you don't need to,' Jan gushed, and turned a pleading look on Jemma. 'Do Luke and I another favour and take Mr Devetzi home, please, Jemma? You know you don't really like parties and he'll be fine with you. Plus, Luke hasn't had the chance to properly speak to David yet.'

Jemma almost laughed. Jan's barefaced cheek never failed to amaze her. She'd opened her mouth to make some non-committal answer when Theo intervened. 'No, thank you, Miss Sutherland. I wouldn't feel happy imposing on your sister in such a way. It's time I left.' And, taking Luke's arm, he apologised for dragging his grandson away. 'I am feeling rather weak.'

Luke wasn't feeling so great himself. For a man who was always in control, it was galling to have to admit he had been completely blindsided by the evening's events. He wanted to talk to Jemma. Who was he kidding? He wanted to do a lot more than *talk* to her. But now wasn't the time or the place. She would keep, he decided, and the quicker he got away from this disastrous party the better.

'Sorry, ladies, but we have to leave,' Luke said. 'Give my apologies to your father and I'll call you later, Jan. No doubt I'll see you again, Jemma.'

Not if I see you first, Jemma thought. Then, while Jan monopolised Luke's attention once more, she leant forward and kissed the old man's cheek. 'You take care, Theo.'

'I will. You've been very kind to me, Jemma. And, disappointed as I am about the villa, I would like to repay your kindness by taking you out to lunch tomorrow, before I return to Greece.'

'I can't tomorrow,' Jemma refused, glad she had a genuine excuse. She had already lied to Theo about not having met Luke before, and she'd rather not have to lie to him again. But as it happened she was lunching with Alan's parents in Eastbourne—something she did every month. 'I'm lunching with my parents-in-law tomorrow; although it's over two years since I lost my husband, we still keep in touch. So some other time, perhaps,' she said quietly.

Much as she liked the old man, she wanted nothing whatsoever to do with his grandson, and the quicker the Devetzi males left, the better she would like it. Jemma heaved a shaky sigh of relief as she watched Theo follow Jan and Luke out into the hall.

'Thanks a bunch,' Jan said sarcastically five minutes later, having returned from escorting the men out. 'You could have insisted on taking the old bloke home, and then Luke could have stayed longer.'

'Maybe—you know Luke Devetzi better than I do,' Jemma said, shrugging. 'But he strikes me as a man who does what he wants, and gets what he wants—women included—and I doubt he would be the faithful type.' It was as near as Jemma felt she could go in warning Jan just what an inveterate womaniser Luke Devetzi was. 'I hope you know what you're getting into.' Jan was selfish, but harmless, and she would hate to see her get hurt.

'That's the problem,' Jan said with her usual bluntness. 'I haven't succeeded in getting into him yet, and I'm dying of frustration. According to the magazines he's been dating Davina Lovejoy, that top New York designer. But he's in London now, and I'm here and she isn't, and surely Luke must be feeling the same. He's notorious for the number of women he's bedded, and for his prowess as a lover.'

It was a lot more than Jemma needed to know, and she burst out laughing. If there was a touch of hysteria in the sound, Jan never noticed.

Two hours later Jemma was back home in the small terraced house in Bayswater she had shared with Alan, curled up in bed.

In his penthouse across town, Luke Devetzi studied Theo with some frustration. His grandfather had never said a word on the drive home. On arriving back at the apartment, Theo had poured them both a nightcap and simply said the villa was not for sale and he was no longer bothered. Now he was sitting on the sofa, his leg once more propped up on a footstool. His dark eyes lacked their usual sparkle, and the expression on his face was one of resigned acceptance.

'Let me get this straight: after all the fuss you have made trying to buy the villa on Zante, now you're telling me you don't care any more?'

'I do care. It's just that I have finally realised it's impossible,' Theo said quietly. 'Jemma explained to me tonight that she can't sell it because her aunt left it in trust for her and her children, and her children's children.'

'Trusts can be broken,' Luke suggested. 'You don't have to give up yet.'

'Maybe.' Theo sighed. 'But it can take years to wade through legal red tape, and even if I live long enough—well, you've met Jemma—can you honestly see a beautiful, compassionate woman like her being a widow for much longer? I can't. She is young, and her husband has been dead for over two years.'

Luke sat down suddenly and almost choked on his whisky. So Jemma had not been married when he'd slept with her! 'Two years, you say? Are you sure?' he queried. He had made enough mistakes with Jemma, and he was determined to make no more. He could almost laugh at how wrong he'd been about her—except that it wasn't funny. His grandfather had lost his dream, and he had bedded and then insulted the sexiest woman he had ever met.

'Yes, she told me tonight as we were leaving. She may not realise it yet, but she has done her mourning. Unless all English men are blind, some guy will snap her up and she will almost certainly be married and with child long before the trust can be broken. It's hopeless, and I am going to bed.' Picking up his stick, he rose to his feet and hobbled up the steps. Stopping at the top, he turned and said, 'Milo and I are going back to Greece in the morning. Goodnight.' And he left.

Luke saw the defeated droop to Theo's shoulders as he left the room. He hated that his grandfather had been disappointed, but he had to admit the old man's assessment was right—getting the villa did look pretty hopeless now.

He saw again in his mind's eye the beautiful Jemma, so calm and considerate with Theo, but so cool with him. His body hardened as he recalled her naked body in every minute detail—the silken softness of her skin, the sweet taste of her rose-tipped breasts, the almost dreamlike quality of their lovemaking which had grown into a white-hot, all-consuming passion.

Restlessly he stood up again, about to pour another whisky. But he stopped. He didn't need a drink; he needed to think. Maybe if he approached Jemma personally and offered her an enormous amount of money to break the trust she would agree. With the exception of his grandmother, he had never met a woman yet who did not love money. And if plan A failed—though he doubted it would—he needed a plan B. He was thirty-seven, past the age most men married. Perhaps it was time to take the plunge and marry. And if by marrying Jemma and producing a child that would also be Theo's geat-grandchild to inherit the villa, then his grandfather would secure his heart's desire—to keep the villa in the family—and that was all the better. Plus, Luke wanted Jemma back in his bed—and he was a man who always got what he wanted.

There was only one huge flaw in plan B. Jemma wouldn't give him the time of day because, apart from him virtually throwing her off his yacht a year ago, she knew he was dating her stepsister. Settling back down on the sofa, his broad brow creased in a frown, he replayed the events of the evening and the information he had gleaned in the last few days. His frown vanished and a predatory smile curved his sensuous mouth. His grey eyes were gleaming with the light of challenge as he rose to his feet and headed for bed. His mind was made up, his course of action determined.

CHAPTER THREE

JEMMA parked her small estate car in a resident's parking space outside her own front door and, picking up her purse and a carrier bag full of garden vegetables from the passenger seat, got out of the car. Straightening up, she stretched her shoulders, her eyes sweeping over the small strip of front garden, which was a mass of colour in the June sun, and sighed contentedly. It had been a long drive to Eastbourne and back, but worth the travel.

She had had a great day; she had helped Sid, her father-in-law, in the garden, and enjoyed a wonderful lunch prepared by his wife Mavis. Then all three of them had taken a walk on the beach, and finally visited Alan's grave. Afterwards they had returned to the house and had tea.

Jemma, her stomach full and her spirit restored by the kindness of Alan's parents, had rationalised on the journey back to London the guilty memories that had kept her awake for hours the night before. Then she'd firmly pushed them back into the darkest corner of her mind, where they belonged.

Luke Devetzi had been a horrendous mistake, brought about by depression and too much wine, and for someone like herself, who had no head for alcohol and rarely drank more than the occasional glass of wine, it wasn't surprising she had acted so out of character—to the point of practically hallucinating.

Totally oblivious to the sleek black car parked twenty yards up the street, Jemma searched in her purse for her door key, happy to be back to the house in Bayswater that

she and Alan had bought when they married. She unlocked the door and walked into the hall. Placing the carrier bag on the floor, she turned to close the door behind
her and let out a strangled yelp.

'May I come in?' Before she could catch her breath
and respond, Luke Devetzi was in her hallway with the
door closed behind him. 'You and I need to talk, Jemma.'
One dark brow lifted wickedly. 'Or perhaps I should call
you Mimie?'

Wide-eyed, she stared up at him, stunned by his totally
unexpected appearance in her home. Then shock and a
fast rising temper made her blush furiously. 'I don't want
you to call me anything; just get the hell out of my house,'
she snapped angrily.

'Such temper! You do surprise me—after all, what
could be more natural when two old friends meet up again
unexpectedly than to have a nice *chat*, as you English
say?' he drawled with cynical amusement.

With a terrific effort of self-control, Jemma forced herself to think clearly. She wished she had never met Luke
Devetzi, and she certainly didn't want to talk to him. All
she really wanted to do was throw him out. But one look
at the grim determination on his attractive face and common sense told her he was far too big and strong, there
was no chance of throwing him anywhere…

He was casually dressed in a tan leather jacket, that fell
smoothly from broad, powerful shoulders, and a white
sports shirt, open at the neck, contrasted sharply with his
tanned skin and the beginning of dark curling chest hair.
The jacket was open, and a hide belt supported pleated
trousers that hugged lean hips, powerful thighs and long
legs. But there was nothing casual about his stance—with
his legs slightly splayed, looming over her, he was awe-
somely male and decidedly threatening.

Refusing to be intimidated in her own home, Jemma stiffened her spine. Tilting her head back, her amber eyes clashed with steel-grey, and she wondered how she had ever thought that Luke's eyes were the same blue as her beloved Alan's had been. She shivered slightly and squashed the unsettling memory. Keep cool, keep calm, she told herself. This was her stepsister's boyfriend and he was nothing to do with her.

'I don't know how you found out where I live, and I don't appreciate you bursting into my home. I have nothing to say to you, and I would like you to leave.'

'Jan told me—in fact she was quite informative—and I'm sorry to disappoint you, Jemma, but I have no intention of leaving until you have answered a few questions,' Luke said smoothly.

Her flash of temper had revealed that she was not as immune to him as she would have him believe. His eyes narrowed speculatively on her beautiful face and then roamed lower over her luscious body. Her shining mass of hair had been caught by a yellow ribbon at the nape of her elegant neck to fall in a long silken banner down her back. She was wearing a buttercup coloured cropped top that clung lovingly to her high breasts, and she was obviously braless, the sweet nipples that tormented his night dreams more often than he cared to admit clearly outlined by the fine cotton. A tempting strip of smooth flesh was revealed as the top barely met the white trousers that clung to her slim hips and legs. On her feet she wore flat sandals, with her cute pink toes on display again. He was definitely a breast and leg man—so when had he developed a foot fetish? Luke wondered wryly as his whole body tensed in an effort to control his over-active libido.

He looked up and saw the flicker of something very

like fear in the golden eyes that met his. Jemma Barnes had good reason to be afraid; she had lied to him about her name, and lied to him about her marriage. He had taken Jan to lunch a few hours ago, to tactfully let her know that he thought of her only as an old friend. She had taken it remarkably well, especially when he'd offered to invest in her agency, and during the conversation that followed, with some subtle questioning, he had discovered from her that Jemma's passion was plants and that for the past two years she had apparently lived the life of a nun. So either Jemma was a great liar, or a great actress, or both.

Trust Jan to open her big mouth, Jemma thought, the silence lengthening as they stared at each other, the tension stretching between them an almost tangible thing. It was Jemma who looked away first.

'In that case,' she said, as she bent down and picked up the bag of vegetables to avoid his too intent gaze. 'You'd better follow me into the kitchen. You can tell me what you have to say while I put these away.' And she walked along the hall, past the stairs, to the back of the house and the kitchen.

She didn't want Luke in her living room—she didn't want him in her house—but the kitchen was suitably impersonal, she figured. Skirting the centrally placed breakfast table, she placed the bag on the bench beneath the window.

The hair on the back of her neck prickled as she sensed Luke's presence behind her. Perhaps the small kitchen had not been such a good idea, she thought as she withdrew the vegetables from the carrier bag. The fridge was on the opposite wall, and reluctantly she turned around, a lettuce in her hand, and came face to face with Luke again.

'Excuse me—I need the fridge,' she said politely.

'You and me both,' Luke said with dry self-mockery, gleaming grey eyes inviting her to share his humour.

But Jemma was not impressed by the *double entendre*. He was only inches away, and she felt at a distinct disadvantage with his great body towering over her. Instinctively she took a step back, and came to a halt against the bench. With nowhere to go, she ignored his innuendo and glanced up at him. 'Then let me pass and I'll get you a cold drink,' she said coolly, with a sarcastic tilt of one delicate brow.

He was too close, his glittering silver gaze too knowing, and suddenly the evocative scent of his cologne reminded her of another time, another place—the close confines of a yacht's cabin. She drew in a deep, unsteady breath. No—she wasn't going there…

'I don't want a cold drink, Jemma,' Luke refused, determined to be reasonable even though his baser instincts were telling him to take her in his arms and kiss her senseless. 'What I want is to discuss the possibility of breaking the trust on the house you own in Zante so my grandfather can buy it. Plus, I want an explanation as to why you told me you were married when we met on the island a year ago.' He paused, a smile quirking the corners of his mouth. 'And I want you, of course…but not necessarily in that order.' He smiled and took the lettuce from her suddenly nerveless fingers and placed it on the bench behind her, then rested his hands on the bench at either side of her shapely body, effectively trapping her.

Keep calm, keep cool. Jemma silently repeated her mantra, but without much success as fear fuelled her temper and she responded angrily. 'Not in any order. There's no question of breaking my aunt's trust—the house can't be sold—and I don't owe you an explanation. In fact, I don't even owe you the time of day, given that you're dating my stepsister. But if you're afraid I might tell Jan of our extremely brief and incredibly unfortunate liaison, let me set your mind at rest. I would rather cut out my tongue than admit to so much as touching you.'

'Then asking you to marry me is out of the question, I take it?' Luke asked, progressing straight to plan B with a hint of amusement in his tone.

'You've got that right! I wouldn't marry a lecherous, womanising swine like you if you were the last man on earth!' Jemma shot back furiously. She lifted her hands to push him away, but as she flattened her palms on his chest she knew she had made a big mistake. His dark head jerked back and all trace of amusement vanished as his eyes, now glittering with silver shards of icy fury, bored into hers.

'If that is your opinion of me, then I have nothing to lose, have I?' he snarled, and two strong arms wrapped around her and hauled her hard against his powerful frame. His dark head swooped suddenly and his sensuous mouth captured hers with a driving passion that owed more to an urge to dominate than to desire.

With her arms pinned to her side, trapped in the cradle of his thighs, she was helpless to escape. She tried to turn her head away from his, but with a speed that overwhelmed her one hand slid up her back and grasped the thick swathe of hair at her nape, holding her immobile beneath his furious onslaught. She felt the fierce tension in every inch of his body, and the thrusting strength of his arousal against her belly. Then, shockingly, as his tongue plundered the moist interior of her mouth, a responding surge of awareness sizzled through her, taking her breath away.

This was what she had tried to banish from her mind for twelve months...what she had been afraid of... The total seduction of her senses… But she was tempted; heat pooled in her pelvis and, helpless to control her traitorous body, she involuntarily swayed into him. Sensing her surrender, he gentled, his tongue teasing and licking with an erotic expertise that sent her already racing pulse into overdrive.

'God, Jemma!' he husked against her mouth, one hand slipping up to stroke across her breasts, his fingers grazing the burgeoning nipples through the soft cotton of her top. 'Or Mimie—whatever you call yourself. I've never forgotten the last time you were in my arms, and I want you again—badly.' His dark head lifted and he fixed her with a piercing silver gaze. 'Say yes.'

It was Luke calling her *Mimie* that shocked Jemma brutally back from the brink of shameful compliance. Only Alan had ever called her Mimie. When Aunt Mary had introduced her to Alan as 'my niece Jemima', Alan had declared it was a bit of a mouthful and so he would call her Mimie—and he had, until the day he died. To hear it on Luke's tongue now seemed like the worst kind of betrayal.

'Don't you *dare* call me Mimie!' she yelled, and with a frantic shove that knocked him back on his heels she wriggled free from his hold. On shaking legs she spun across the kitchen to put the width of the breakfast table between them. Flushed and furious, and with her heart pounding madly, she grasped the back of one of the pine chairs to steady herself.

Luke turned around and leant casually back against the bench. He saw her white-knuckled grip on the chair, the anger and the fear in her huge eyes, and cursed under his breath. He should never have pounced on her so fiercely. But she had enraged him with her estimation of his character and he had completely lost control, which was most unlike him.

'A simple "no" would have done, Jemma,' he drawled. Why she objected to the name Mimie he was determined to discover. But now was not the time. 'I've never had to pressure a woman into bed and I don't intend to start with you, so you can relax your grip on the chair and get me that drink you offered.'

'The drink I offered?' Jemma echoed in an incredulous tone, the nerve of the man astounding her. 'Are you crazy? I want you out of my house *now*.'

'Now, is that any way to treat a guest?' Luke straightened and strolled forward. 'Think what your father would say if he heard his daughter had behaved with such an appalling lack of manners to the grandson of one of his major shareholders. Then there's Jan as well, as you were so kind to point out.' He stopped beside her, his grey eyes narrowing on her flushed face.

'My father…Jan…?' Jemma repeated. What was he going on about? And why did she have the uneasy feeling there was a threat in there somewhere?

'Jan is under the impression—along with everyone else—that you're one step removed from a saint and have lived the life of a nun since the death of your husband. So, as for you not telling her about our one-night stand— that you would *cut out your tongue* rather than tell her, I believe you said—well, I have no such qualms. I will quite happily tell the whole world I made love to you last year. Though it might spoil your grieving widow act somewhat.'

His callous comment hurt her deeply—her grief was not an act. Jemma missed her late husband every day; she missed his kindness, his comfort, his conversation, and the sense of absolute love and security that Alan had provided. Yet this arrogant, conceited jerk, who had probably never loved anyone in his life, had the nerve to mock her loss.

Luke's deriding of her grief transformed her hurt into a cold, defiant anger. Releasing her grip on the chair, slowly Jemma turned and squared her shoulders. 'You would do that? You would deliberately upset Jan in that way? Now, why doesn't that surprise me?' she jeered, giving a disgusted shake of her head. Not waiting for his response, she added, 'Follow me and I'll get you that drink.' Completely ignoring him, she walked out of the kitchen and opened the door into the living room, knowing exactly what he would see.

She crossed to a small antique bureau that doubled as a drinks cabinet and filled a crystal glass with a shot of whisky.

'I only have whisky, I'm afraid.' She turned and walked back to where Luke was standing, looking curiously around. 'Here.' She held out the glass and made sure her fingers did not touch his as he took it from her with a brief 'Thanks' and a knowing lift of one dark brow that simply reinforced her determination to be rid of him once and for all.

'It's a very good Irish malt, I believe.. not that I drink it,' she continued, crossing to sit down on one of the large sofas that framed the ornate Victorian fireplace. 'But it was Alan's favourite and he was quite a connoisseur. Now, remind me, what was it you thought so urgent that you had to barge into my house to talk to me?' She watched as he prowled around the room, glass in hand. The room she had thought was spacious suddenly seemed to take on the dimensions of a doll's house with Luke Devetzi's presence, and as the silence lengthened she shifted uncomfortably and finally added, 'Please take a seat.'

'I'd rather stand, thank you.' One look around the room had been enough to tell Luke the place was a virtual shrine to the late, lamented Alan Barnes… He picked up a framed wedding photograph from among the dozen or more framed photographs arranged on top of a beautifully inlaid console table and grimaced. The bride was Jemma, and she was gazing up into the face of her groom with a totally besotted smile on her face. The tender but triumphant smile on the man's face said it all. The fact that he was quite good-looking, with brown curly hair and laughing blue eyes, did nothing to improve Luke's mood. 'You were a beautiful bride,' he said finally, glancing across at her. She calmly nodded her head in thanks but said not word.

He put the picture back down and glanced over the others. There was a group photo of the wedding; it had obviously been a big affair. There were more pictures of the happy couple with a crowd of friends at a barbecue, and one of Jemma at her husband's side by a swimming pool, holding his hand and laughing. The image of a near naked Jemma in a tiny bikini darkened his mood still further.

Frowning, he abruptly turned away and took a swallow of the whisky; there was no denying it was good malt. But he was drinking another man's whisky, lusting after a dead man's wife, and somehow it left a nasty taste in his mouth. He strolled back to where Jemma sat watching him with cool, guarded eyes and lowered his long frame down on the sofa opposite her.

'Your husband was an attractive man; how long had you known him before you married?' Luke asked, not really sure why. But Jemma fascinated him in a way no woman had in years—if ever, he wryly conceded. Serene and beautiful she might be on the outside, but he knew she was a burning cauldron of passion within.

'You want a potted history of my life? Then will you get out of it?' she demanded bluntly.

'If that is what you want…yes.' Luke agreed.

Taking him at his word, Jemma launched into speech. 'I met Alan when I was twelve and he was twenty-one, working for my aunt Mary as a researcher. He became my best friend, and later my boyfriend when I was at college. He encouraged my interest in floristry, and when I graduated he encouraged me to set up in business with Liz. He was kind, loving, and totally supportive. We married when I was twenty-two. Four years later he was killed in a gliding accident.'

'He might have been a paragon of virtue, but he was also a fool to risk his life gliding with a passionate, sexy woman like you at home to warm his bed,' Luke murmured.

She didn't like the 'passionate, sexy' bit, that was not Jemma at all, but she let nothing show on her face as she responded coolly, 'You never knew him, so your opinion is irrelevant.'

'Was he a passionate lover?'

'That's none of your business,' she snapped, outraged that he dared ask. 'And now I've told you what you wanted to know, will you please leave?'

'Surely I'm allowed to finish my whisky first?' He raised his glass to her, then took a sip and lounged back on the sofa, stretching his long legs out before him with nonchalant ease.

Jemma might have guessed it had been too good to be true when he'd agreed to leave so readily. She hoped the whisky choked the damn man. But with a patently false smile she said sweetly, 'If you must.'

'Thank you. I must say your husband did have great taste in whisky—among other things,' Luke taunted, allowing his eyes to roam slowly over her in blatant masculine appraisal of her gorgeous body.

She was sitting there so prim, so cool, and yet he knew she was anything but... Her back was ramrod-straight, her arms were folded across her lush breasts and her knees were pressed tightly together. If she'd been any more on the defensive she would have been carrying a shield and sword. He wondered why... She wasn't a young girl— she had to be twenty-eight, by his reckoning—and she was certainly no virgin, so why was she intent on denying the sexual chemistry between them?

'Have you slept with any other man besides me since your husband died?' he asked, and saw the flash of temper in the golden depths of her eyes.

'Certainly not,' Jemma said without thinking.

'I see—so why me?' Luke asked, holding her angry gaze with his own. 'I'm entitled to know, Jemma—after all, it's not every day a man picks up a beautiful woman and makes love to her, and then afterwards she slips a wedding ring on her finger and declares that she is married.'

'Decent men don't pick up women,' she bit out, amazed at his effrontery in asking so many personal questions.

'By the same token decent women don't allow themselves to be picked up,' Luke retorted dryly. 'So that makes us two of a kind, wouldn't you say?'

Jemma blushed at his insulting comment. 'I would prefer not to say anything to you at all,' she shot back, but she could not deny his reasoning.

'Unfortunately that's not an option; I have no intention

of leaving here until I discover what made you sleep with me—other than my undoubted charm, of course,' he said with a grin. 'As I recall you came into my arms and my bed willingly, and what followed was a wildly passionate and mutual satisfying encounter for both of us. I've rarely met a more compatible woman in the bedroom, so why the lies about your name, your married status?'

There was a long silence as they stared at each other, the air in the room heavy with the tension of two people who had shared a brief, fiercely physical episode. Jemma was trying her best to forget it had ever happened, even as an unwanted heat surged under every inch of her skin at the memory. As for being compatible with him on any level, her heart shrank at the notion, and she tore her gaze from his to focus on the window behind him, the evening sun streaming through the glass panes blinding her for a moment.

Jemma blinked; she had absolutely nothing in common with a super-rich sophisticated giant of the financial world like Luke Devetzi. Hers had been a typical middle class upbringing, comfortably provided for by a small family business. It was only after her father had married again that the house she had known as home all her life had been traded in for the lavish house in Connaught Square, at her stepmother's instigation, and that the company had expanded in leaps and bounds and the family had become very wealthy, according to her dad. Not that Jemma had noticed—she worked for her living.

'I asked you a question,' Luke prompted sharply. He could tell by the expression on her beautiful face that her thoughts had drifted away from him, and he didn't like it at all… 'Why did you lie?'

The demand in his deep voice finally captured Jemma's attention. Thinking about the past was not helping her present situation, she realized, and her own common sense told her Luke was never going to let her forget or leave her alone until he had an explanation.

Rising slowly to her feet, she glanced down at him. 'Okay, I'll make a deal with you. I'll tell you what you want to know.' Her own innate honesty urged her to tell him the truth and shame the devil, and finally draw a line under the horrendous event once and for all. 'But you have to promise to leave and never bother me again—no more excuses.'

'Fair enough,' Luke agreed smoothly.

She wasn't convinced his word could be trusted, but she gave him the benefit of the doubt—mainly because she could see no other way of getting rid of him. Jemma walked across the room and picked up her favourite picture of Alan from the console table, then returned to her seat on the sofa. She looked at the photo for a while, and then, lifting her head, saw Luke had leant back on the sofa again and was watching her with hard, intelligent eyes.

'The day I met you would have been my fourth wedding anniversary,' she said flatly. She saw him grimace and knew she had scored a hit. 'But it wasn't just that. It was a culmination of…' she paused for a moment '…disasters, if you like. I had arrived on Zante two weeks earlier with my aunt, at her insistence; it was the first time I had visited the island, and in fact I didn't even know Aunt Mary had a home there. For various reasons she wanted me to go with her—the main one being she'd been told a month earlier she had a very limited time left to live. Naturally I was upset, and as it happened she died a few months later from asbestosis.'

Jemma drifted from the point, her amber eyes darkening with remembered sorrow. 'Odd, but I'd always

thought of asbestosis as an industrial disease only afflict-
ing men. But Aunt Mary reckoned she probably con-
tracted it working in laboratories decades ago, where the
perceived form of protection against fire was asbestos lin-
ing in the ceilings and walls. Anyway, it wasn't the happiest of holidays,' she continued, 'but we did try to enjoy
ourselves, and I built her the rockery she had always
wanted. In the process I dropped a stone on my hand.
Three of my fingers were badly swollen, and my wedding
ring had to be cut off.' She looked at Luke, her expressive
face bleak. 'I took it to a shop in the town to be repaired,
and when I met you I had just retrieved it from the jew-
ellers. I had tried to put it back on in the shop, but my
finger was still a little swollen. You wouldn't understand,
having never been married, but I was upset.

'I don't usually drink, but I ordered a glass of wine
from the bar while I waited for the local bus and the
waiter brought a carafe instead. I had a couple of glasses,
maybe more, and I was thinking about Alan and our wedding day when the accident with the wine happened and
you appeared.' She stopped and, leaning forward, she very
deliberately offered him the photo. 'Take a look.' He took
it from her outstretched hand without comment.

'That's my favourite photo of Alan, and when I looked
up into your eyes that day—so blue and so concerned,
just like Alan's—and you asked me my name, in my be-
fuddled state I said Mimie, because that was what Alan
always called me. Then in a daze of sadness and confusion I simply followed where you led. I admit I behaved
badly, and by the time I came to my senses I was horrified. Perhaps it was the reflection of the water or something.' A puzzled frown briefly marred her smooth brow.
'Because actually your eyes are nothing like Alan's—
yours are grey, like granite,' she said with a glance at

him. Seeing the thunderous frown on his face, she realised she was digressing. 'Anyway, I dashed into the bathroom, got dressed, and forced my ring back on my finger. You know the rest.'

'My God!' Luke exclaimed, white hot fury engulfing him. To hear this woman he had made love to say she had been horrified afterwards was bad enough, but as for the rest…! 'You expect me to believe you slept with me because I reminded you of your husband?' he demanded scathingly. And, dropping the picture, he leapt to his feet and crossed the space dividing them. 'I look nothing like the man,' he snarled.

He had never been so insulted in his life, and he was damned if he was going to let Jemma get away with such a damaging blow to his pride. Angrily he studied her, his eyes raking over her body. The cotton top she was wearing was pulled tight across her high, firm breasts as she perched on the edge of the sofa, her hands clenched into the soft fabric either side of her like some exotic bird ready for flight.

Shocked by the extent of his fury, Jemma saw the dark flush across his high cheekbones, the icy glitter in his eyes, and too late realised it had probably not been the best idea in the world to tell such an arrogant man the truth.

A man with an ego the size of Luke Devetzi's wasn't exactly going to be pleased to discover he had been used as a stand-in for another man. It was ironic, in a way, and the briefest of dry smiles curved her lips as she recalled Jan telling her how Luke was renowned for using women. But, discretion being the better part of valour, Jemma didn't voice her thoughts; instead she slipped along the sofa and stood up, as far away from him as she could get. 'I didn't say you looked like him. I said your eyes appeared blue—a trick of the light.' She attempted to mollify him. 'But it's not important now, because you promised to leave me alone if I told you the truth, and I have.' As far as Jemma was concerned she had kept her part of the deal and she wanted him gone.

'Oh, I'm leaving all right.' Luke stepped towards her, and for a moment Jemma thought her ordeal was over and he was going. 'But first I'm going to prove to you that you're fooling no one but yourself.' And before she could react to his outrageous statement, he reached for her and pulled her against his hard body, his sensuous mouth capturing hers with punishing ferocity.

CHAPTER FOUR

FOR a heartbeat she was frozen in shock as he tried to force her lips apart. But only for a heartbeat. Not again, Jemma vowed, incandescent with rage at his caveman tactics and his total disregard of his promise to leave. Curling her hand into a fist, she lashed out at him and brought her knee up hard, aiming for the most vulnerable part of the man. With lightening reflexes he jerked away. But, caught off balance, he fell back and took her with him and they landed in a tangled heap on the sofa.

Winded, and before she knew what had happened, Jemma was flat on her back, with the weight of his body pinning her down. She tried to lash out at him again, but he caught her hands and secured them firmly above her head with one of his.

'Oh, no, you don't,' he grated. 'I won't tolerate violence from anyone, and certainly not from a she-devil like you.'

'What do you call this, then?' she cried, trying to wriggle from beneath him. But in reaction to her movement she felt the hardening potency of his masculine arousal against her thigh and realised her mistake. The last thing she needed was a rampant, raging Luke—the heat that suffused her own body she put down to temper.

His hard mouth curved in a lethal smile. 'A lesson in how to greet your lover,' he rasped, and she knew he was going to kiss her. She whipped her head to one side to avoid him, and his mouth closed over the rapidly beating pulse in her neck. She gasped as his firm lips trailed up to her ear. Blowing gently, he added, 'Because, however much you wish it wasn't true, I am your last lover. Not your long-dead husband.'

Fury at his comment battled with a rising tide of excitement that she fought to control. She wanted to deny him, but the warmth of his breath in her ear, the familiar male scent of him, the weight of his body on hers, evoked a multitude of memories she had sternly suppressed.

With finger and thumb Luke grasped her chin and turned her face to his. 'You know I'm right,' he murmured, and his teeth nipped at her lower lip, demanding that she give him access and abandon herself to the sensual awareness that had simmered beneath the surface between them ever since they had met again last night.

Later she would realise just how cunning he had been, but now, as he stroked his tongue gently across her lips, she ached to give in to his erotic demand and lose herself in the heady pleasure of his kiss. Still she tried to resist the shattering sexual impact of his mouth, teasing and tasting hers, and she might have succeeded if he had remained forcible, but he was too experienced a lover to be so crass. And when his hand dropped from her chin to slip up beneath her cotton top and cup one firm breast, an arrow of excitement shot from her breast to her groin.

Her lips parted involuntarily and his tongue probed the soft, moist interior with an eroticism that aroused an answering passion in her she battled to control…and failed. His fingers found the pert pink tip of one breast and plucked gently, bringing it to a tight, hard nub of aching desire before stroking across to deliver the same exquisite pleasure to the other. And all the time his sensual mouth devoured hers in a kiss of ever-deepening desire.

His head lifted and a low moan escaped her. As though it was a signal Luke had been waiting for, he released her wrists and pulled her top over her head. Blinded for a moment, when Jemma opened her eyes it was to see Luke, minus his jacket, staring down at her body with intent, hungry eyes. Then his dark head dipped and he kissed her again, before placing kisses down her throat and then lower, his tongue teasingly circling a swollen nipple, slowly drawing the rigid tip between his teeth to suckle it.

Jemma's back arched in helpless response as a feverish excitement rocketed through her body. It had been too long since she had been in a man's arms—in *this* man's arms—since she had felt the exquisite pleasure of sexual arousal, and Luke had seduced her utterly. One small hand slipped beneath the open neck of his shirt to cling to his broad shoulder, the other curving around the nape of his neck, her fingers combing involuntarily through the silky black hair of his head and urging him closer to her aching breasts. Jemma's eyelids drifted down in helpless response to his expert touch and she gave herself up completely, to revel in the exquisite sensations consuming her whole body. She felt his hand on her belly and had no idea when he had unzipped her trousers. But she didn't care as his long fingers slipped beneath her lace panties to cup the mound of her sex.

Luke raised his head, his molten silver gaze burning over her near-naked body. She was everything he remembered and so much more, and his own hunger threatened to explode as he saw her beautiful face flushed with passion, her glorious eyes…closed…

Luke growled deep in his throat and reared back. 'Open your eyes, Jemma,' he demanded harshly. Her thick lashes lifted and she stared up at him, her golden gaze hazed with desire. With one long finger he outlined her pouting mouth. 'Now, say my name.'

'Luke,' she murmured breathlessly, and tried to push his shirt from his shoulders.

'And again,' he insisted, dipping his head to lave and then briefly nip the peak of first one breast and then the other before returning to take her mouth once more. He felt her body jerk up beneath him and he ached to be inside her, hard and fast and immediately... 'My name, Jemma,' he demanded yet again.

'Luke,' she groaned. 'Luke, don't stop...'

'Good. Very good,' he grated between suddenly clenched teeth, and with superhuman control he forced himself to grasp her shoulders and push her back against the sofa, to rise to his feet.

Jemma looked up at Luke with passion-dazed eyes and involuntarily lifted a hand towards him. She felt the cool air against her breasts, but it was as nothing to the coldness in the gaze that swept briefly over her reclining form.

'But stop we must, because although we have established that you say my name so eagerly, you will never mistake me for your husband or any other man again.'

Jemma shivered at the implacable tone in his voice. Something had gone wrong. Instinctively she edged up into a sitting position.

'And, beautiful and wanton though you are—' he reached out and brushed a few tendrils of hair from her brow '—I have no intention of making love to you in this shrine to your dead husband.' His silkily voiced comment acted like a bucket of iced water on Jemma's overheated senses. 'The next time we make love will be at a place and time of my choosing, Jemma.'

She stared up at his shuttered face, unwilling to believe what her mind was telling her was true. She recognised the gleam of cynical triumph in his steel-grey eyes, the dark desire in the enlarged black pupils, and turned her head away. He had deliberately made love to her for no other reason than as a sop to his monumental ego. How could she have been so dumb? Such a push-over?

Desire and disgust fought inside her. Her shattered gaze lighted on the picture of Alan on the sofa opposite, and somehow it gave her strength. She took a deep, shuddering breath, and then another. She wouldn't let Luke know how easily he could reduce her to the wanton he had called her; she wouldn't give him the satisfaction. Instead she would play him at his own game.

'Nice thought.' She forced a smile to her swollen lips and slid off the sofa. Picking up her top, she added, 'You're right. This isn't the place.' She pulled her top over her head and smoothed it over her breasts, taking her time to regain some semblance of control before glancing up at him. If she had not been so bitterly ashamed and angry she might have laughed at the expression of surprise on his face. He had obviously not expected her to agree with him. 'Thank you for reminding me.. and, speaking of time, it's time you left.'

Gathering every scrap of will-power she could muster, she sauntered towards the door and had stepped about three paces along the hall before Luke caught up with her. Taking her arm, he turned her around to face him, a querying light in his shrewd grey eyes.

'You're suddenly being very reasonable.'

'Why not?' Jemma casually shrugged her shoulders and brushed his hand from her arm, opening the front door. In seconds she had walked down the short garden path and stepped out onto the pavement, and turned to find he was right behind her. Bravely she looked him in the eye, though she was shaking inside with humiliation and rage. 'After all, you and I both know it's never going to happen.

Because you're incapable of making love,' she jeered softly.

'Incapable!' Luke repeated in amazement. 'Whatever gave you that idea? Don't tell me.' He answered his own question. 'It's your frustration talking, because I wouldn't make love to you just now.' Why did this woman feel the need to insult his sexual prowess when she knew perfectly well that she was putty in his arms any time he chose? He shook his head in exasperation. Jemma was the most infuriating female he had ever met. He really didn't need someone like her in his well-ordered life when he knew without conceit that he could take his pick from dozens of much more amenable women. And how the hell had she manoeuvred him out onto the pavement?

Jemma saw him stiffen in outrage and she didn't give a damn. It was way past time the arrogant devil heard a few home truths. 'No, it's not frustration talking, just the simple truth,' she stated bluntly. 'You don't make love— you have sex, and lots of it, with countless women, by all accounts. But I suppose, given your great wealth, that's to be expected. To give you your due, you do appear to know all the right buttons to press,' she declared with a humourless smile, and added, 'But you do lack a lot in the sensitivity stakes. And, since I have known real love, I'm never going to settle for anything less,' she concluded, not bothering to hide the utter contempt in her tone.

Luke wanted to grab her by the shoulders and shake her till her teeth rattled. He was enraged at the brutal dissection of his character—although a part of his anger was with himself, because he could not totally deny what Jemma had said. He drew in a deep, harsh breath, fighting to control his temper.

'You say that now, Jemma, but never is a very long

time.' He smiled unpleasantly. 'And you may not have a choice.'

'One always has a choice,' Jemma asserted, and almost added *And I would never choose you,* but, glancing up at him, she saw the threat in his eyes, in the powerful body looming over her, and she held her tongue as a sliver of apprehension ran down her spine.

'True… But sometimes the choice is not between good and bad, right and wrong.' His grey eyes held hers, a calculating and sinister light in the glittering depths. 'Often it's between the lesser of two evils, as you will no doubt learn.'

Jemma watched Luke shrug on his jacket, and with a last contemptuous glance at her he spun on his heel and walked away. She saw him step into a racy black car parked a few metres along the pavement. He never looked back.

A long drawn out sigh escaped her. Luke had gone— thank God! She had got rid of the man at last, and she should have felt relieved. But instead, as she walked back into the house, all she could feel was a lingering sense of apprehension, and all she could see was his contemptuous expression as he'd left. And what had he meant by *she might not have a choice*?

Half an hour later, having tidied up the living room and made a cup of tea, Jemma sat down on the sofa and sipped the reviving brew. She looked around at all the familiar furnishings and photos, everything that made the room her sanctuary, but oddly it did not give her the same sense of comfort that it usually did. It was as though the alien presence of Luke Devetzi had upset the balance somehow.

No—she was just being fanciful! Picking up the remote for the television, she switched on the history channel and tried to concentrate on a brilliant documentary about Ancient Egypt.

She gave up after ten minutes and wandered around the room, touching her much-loved mementos but still feeling on edge. She headed upstairs. A relaxing bath and then an early night was what she needed. It was her turn to go to the flower market at five the following morning.

Two hours later she was in the king-sized bed she had shared with Alan, but sleep eluded her. She stirred restlessly, finally turning to lie flat on her back, staring blankly at the ceiling. She lifted a finger to her slightly swollen lips, and to her shame it was Luke's kiss that she recalled. Flickering images of their past encounters spun haphazardly through her brain.

Her shock at seeing Luke's darkly attractive face last night at the party was overlaid by a vivid mental image of his magnificent naked body as he knelt between her thighs on another bed in another country. Heat flooded through her, and she groaned and turned over to bury her head in the pillow in an attempt to block out the memories. But it was no good. The past had come back to haunt her in the shape of one Luke Devetzi.

Thinking about him now, she realised it had been a peculiar trick of fate that had brought herself and Luke together. The death of her husband a year earlier and the imminent death of her much-loved aunt coupled with her disappointment over her wedding ring, and then the final blow, when those louts had knocked wine all over her. In her distress she had lifted a tear-glazed gaze to her rescuer, and, because she had so much wanted it to be, she had imagined it was the blue eyes of her husband that smiled back at her.

Later, Luke had shown her to a luxurious cabin and, taking a silk robe from a closet, had dropped it on the bed with the words, 'Strip out of your stained clothes and have a shower, use the robe. I will be back later to collect your clothes and have someone clean them for you.'

Like an automaton, Jemma had agreed. Ten minutes later she'd walked out of the shower room and back into the cabin, wearing only white lace panties and with her dirty clothes in one hand. She'd reached for the robe on the bed just as a knock had sounded on the door and Luke had walked in. He'd said something in Greek she hadn't understood, but the mesmerising effect of his eyes had seemed to paralyse her, and when he'd walked towards her, cupped her chin in one lean hand and said almost reverently, 'You are so beautiful, Mimie,' she had made no demur.

Thinking about it now, Jemma realised with hindsight that she had been in a state of shock. No man but Alan had ever seen her almost naked. And no man but Alan had ever called her Mimie or told her she was beautiful. So it was hardly surprising that when Luke had kissed her with a piercing, sweet tenderness she had responded.

Stirring restlessly in the bed, Jemma groaned out loud. However much she tried to deny it, what had happened next with Luke had been nothing like what she had experienced with her husband.

Luke's hands had caressed her body and shaped her breasts, his tongue thrusting between her parted lips, igniting a consuming heat that had sent shock waves crashing through her body. When he'd finally broken the kiss to speedily strip his clothes from his body she had stood trembling violently, her amber eyes roaming in helpless fascination over his magnificent bronzed frame. Before she'd had time to recover her senses he had lifted her in his arms, whispering huskily voiced endearments as he lowered her to the bed.

The passion had exploded between them with the next touch of his mouth on hers, and in a fever of kisses and caresses Luke had made love to her with a wildly erotic, powerful passion that she had mindlessly returned. She had closed her eyes to the world, and for a while her world had been the man whose arms had enfolded her, whose body had desired hers. They had touched and tasted each other in a frenzy of need that had finally culminated in a wondrous climax that left them both sweat slicked, sated and fighting to breathe.

Thinking about that night now was too much for Jemma, and, giving up any hope of sleep, she slipped out of bed and padded downstairs to the kitchen to make a cup of hot milk.

Everything would look better in the morning, she told herself. Luke Devetzi was gone, and he was never likely to come back after the way she had insulted him. And, given that he was Jan's boyfriend, what was the worst that could happen? If Jemma ever bumped into him on the few occasions she visited her father's house she need exchange nothing with him beyond polite social niceties.

CHAPTER FIVE

LUGGING the last box of flowers from the back of her estate car, Jemma staggered into the shop and put the box down, heaving a sigh of relief. Much as she liked choosing blooms in the flower market, she was not mad about getting up at the crack of dawn. Still, it was a job well done, Jemma told herself, and headed for the bench that contained two sinks and a kettle and much-needed coffee.

The five a.m. start had not been a problem this morning, because she had barely slept last night, but it was catching up with her now. Thankfully she sat down at the desk and took a refreshing swallow of coffee. Everything looked much better in the clear light of day. She had her business, her friends, her own house and small garden, and after a disastrous weekend she was back to normal, with Luke Duvetzi out of her life for good. Draining the mug, she got to her feet and set about unpacking her purchases. Some she put in buckets of water, others she placed on the shelves that lined one wall of the room.

By the time Liz arrived, at nine, Jemma had redesigned the window display and the shop was open for business.

'The place looks great,' Liz declared, and crossed to where Jemma stood propping up the counter. 'But you look like hell.'

'Thanks a bunch,' Jemma shot back 'No pun intended.' She tried to joke in the hope of diverting Liz from the questions that would surely follow.

'I know I said it was time you began to live a little, but you look as if you have burnt the candle at both ends and eaten the middle! Waxen springs to mind... It must have been one heck of a birthday party.' Liz chuckled. 'Come on—tell all. It's the only way this harassed mum gets a thrill these days.'

Jemma knew Liz adored her husband Peter, and her two-year-old son Thomas, and wouldn't change her lifestyle for the world, and she grinned back. 'You're a fibber and there's nothing to tell. It was Dad and Leanne's usual crowd, and I left early at about ten. End of story.'

'You're not fobbing me off like that! At least tell me what Jan's new man looks like. Name, rank, and serial womanizer? Or serious prospect in the marriage stakes?' Liz queried cheekily. 'Fit and handsome or old and fat? The money is a given, knowing Jan.'

Jemma knew Liz wouldn't shut up until she had the full story, but on this occasion she had no intention of telling her everything...

'Tall, dark, and not bad-looking; not old—mid to late thirties, I guess. As for being a marriage prospect, I very much doubt it. He looked like the womanising type to me. But Jan is certainly smitten, and he is filthy rich.'

'And his name is...?'

'Luke something—Devetzi, I think.' She didn't want to seem too sure, as Liz had a nose like a bloodhound when it came to digging out secrets.

'Oh, my God! I don't believe it.' Liz exclaimed. 'You met *the* Luke Devetzi—the financial wizard, the international banker? Not bad-looking! Are you blind, Jemma? The man is a serious hunk. But you're right about the womanising; I've seen his photograph dozens of times in the top magazines, usually with a stunning woman on his arm. I don't fancy Jan's chances of dragging him to the altar; he's definitely not the settling-down type. But, hey—' Liz winked '—Jan's still a very lucky girl to get a man like that in her bed for her birthday. I wouldn't mind him as a present for a night.'

'Liz, you're disgraceful—and you a married woman,' Jemma quipped, but inside she felt sick. How come Liz and apparently the whole world had heard of Luke Devetzi? She hadn't known him from Adam and had stupidly fallen into bed with him. Still, on the up side, after what Liz had just told her she need have no fear of Luke seeking her out. An undeniably attractive, incredibly wealthy man with a world of fawning women to choose from was never going to bother Jemma again.

'I can dream, can't I?' Liz said, her dark eyes twinkling wickedly.

'Dreaming won't get the dozen or so orders done—which we have to deliver before noon,' Jemma said dryly.

'Okay, okay,' Liz agreed. 'You look like you need some help.' She frowned. 'Are you sure you're all right?'

'Yes, fine. But I drove down to Eastbourne and back yesterday, and then with the early start this morning...' She explained with a shrug.

'Say no more. That explains everything—you've visited Alan's parents and his grave.' Liz put her arm around Jemma and gave her a consoling hug. And Jemma felt the biggest fraud imaginable.

The mid-morning sun glinted on the Thames as Jemma drove across Tower Bridge. It was the last day in August—a perfect summer's day and, as it happened, her father's birthday. A contented sigh escaped her. She had spent the last hour in a meeting with the purchasing manager of an upmarket department store on Kensington High Street, and had secured a contract to supply the floral displays for the premises—subject to Liz checking the fine print. Ray would have to concentrate more on floristry, and they would probably have to employ a full time van driver, but already Jemma could see Flower Power gaining much bigger contracts.

Work was going great, and Jemma was looking forward to a private lunch with her father. She had booked a table at an exclusive restaurant as part of his birthday present, and she was picking him up at noon. She would still have to show her face at the party Leanne had organised for tonight, but she wasn't worried—no one would notice if she left early.

She grimaced as she parked the car and glanced up at the impressive façade of the house in Connaught Square. Jan's birthday party here over two months ago had been a disaster as far as she was concerned, but that was all behind her now. She hadn't seen Jan since, but that wasn't so unusual, and Jemma did keep in touch with the family by telephone.

Dismissing the past from her mind, she slid out of the car. She straightened the lapels of the short sleeved cream silk jacket, which fitted neatly over her shoulders and nipped in at her narrow waist, and smoothed the fabric of the slim-fitting skirt down over her hips. It wasn't often she dressed up, preferring casual clothes, but over the years she had built up a collection of classic clothes for when the occasion arose—like today. Brimming with confidence, she knew she looked good, and with purse in hand she ran lightly up the stone steps to the front door.

She let herself in, her high heels clicking jauntily on the marble-tiled floor as she walked down the hall. 'Good morning, Maggie,' she greeted the housekeeper, who was at the foot of the staircase with an empty tray in her hands. 'Where is Dad—still in his study?' she asked, and got the strangest look back.

'No. Yes. I mean he's upstairs, in the first floor drawing room, waiting for you.'

Jemma glanced at her wristwatch; it was only eleven thirty. 'I don't believe it—Dad's early for once. What do you think, Maggie, is the big six-O finally getting to him?' She smiled at Maggie, but got no answering smile back.

'Don't ask me. I only work here.' And she walked away.

What's rattled her cage? Jemma wondered as she walked up the stairs and opened the drawing room door. Maggie was usually the most affable of women.

Her father was sitting in his favourite high-backed chair at one side of the ornate fireplace, a cup of coffee in his hand. 'Happy birthday, Dad.' Jemma grinned and took a couple of steps in his direction.

'Thank you,' he muttered, giving her a weak smile back and then lowering his eyes. Not the most enthusiastic reception she had ever had, Jemma thought, and then stopped, the hair on the back of her neck standing on end. Warily she glanced around the room, and realised they were not alone...

The man was standing with his back to the window. Silhouetted by the morning sun. She wasn't able to see his face clearly, but she didn't need to. It was Luke Devetzi. Her heart leapt, her amber eyes widening to their fullest extent in shock.

'Good morning, Jemma.'

'G...G... Good morning,' she stammered, and simply stared as he moved towards her. He was dressed in a tailored charcoal-grey business suit, white shirt and blue tie. His hair was longer than the last time they had met, but otherwise he was still the same darkly handsome, arrogant man she remembered. She wished she didn't.

'It's a pleasure to meet you again,' he said silkily, and smiled.

She glanced up, and he returned her look with eyes that held no trace of humour, just a remorseless intensity that set warning bells ringing in her head. Her confidence took a nosedive, and she just knew Luke was a danger to her peace of mind.

Jemma shot a nervous glance at her father, but he was no help—he was staring into his coffee cup as though his life depended on it. Something was seriously wrong…

No, she was letting her imagination get the better of her. Luke was no danger to her. He was Jan's friend, she reminded herself. She had always known she might bump into him again in that capacity, and now it had happened—no big deal. Her confidence restored, she broke the lengthening silence. 'Nice to see you again, Luke. But I'm taking my father out for lunch so we can't stop and chat,' she said lightly. 'But do take a seat, make yourself at home; I'm sure Jan won't be long.' Congratulating herself on the cool, mature way she had handled the situation, she did not see the glance that passed between the two men.

'Jemma doesn't know, Sutherland?' At the sound of her own name Jemma glanced up at Luke. He was staring at her father, an expression of disgust on his face. 'You haven't told her?'

'Told me what?' Jemma asked, totally confused.

Granite-grey eyes flicked her way. 'I'm not here to see Jan. I am here to see you—among other things,' Luke offered by way of explanation, before turning his attention back to her father. 'Well, have you, Sutherland?'

'I hadn't the heart, Luke. I told you, Jemma knows nothing about the business, and she wouldn't understand anyway.'

'What wouldn't I understand?' she demanded, turning her puzzled gaze to her father, surprised and hurt that he had demeaned her intelligence in front of Luke so casually.

'I think you'd better sit down, Jemma.' Luke's hand closed around her forearm and she nearly jumped out of her skin at his touch.

'No!' She tried to shake him off, but his grip tightened, and rather than start an ungainly struggle in front of her father she allowed him to lead her to the sofa facing the fireplace.

'Sit down,' he commanded. 'Because believe me, Jemma, you're going to need to,' he murmured very close to her ear—so close she could feel the warmth of his breath against her skin.

'Dad?' She appealed to her father. 'What is—?'

'Do as Luke says and sit down; I have something to tell you.' With a close look at her father's haggard face she complied, sinking down on the sofa with an icy feeling of dread permeating her body. And it didn't help that Luke lowered his long length down beside her.

'You know I love you, Jemma,' her father said softly. 'And I would never do anything to harm you. But unfortunately over the past few years I have made one or two bad business choices. The company is no longer profitable and…'

She listened in mounting horror as her father spoke, and when he had finished she stared at him, ashen faced. Apparently not only had he made a few bad decisions, he had been borrowing money from the firm for years. And since floating the company on AIM and acquiring shareholders outside of the family, the firm's accountancy methods had been called into question by those same shareholders. An independent accountancy firm had been hired. Her father had hoped he could pay back the loans over time, but time had run out. He admitted the last stock flotation had not really been to expand in America but to plug the hole in the accounts.

'I can't believe it. How could you, Dad?' she asked, glancing wildly around the room. And she knew the answer. Leanne had very expensive tastes—this house, for one, as well as the villa in Majorca. She also knew her father had financed the setting up of Jan's modelling agency last year. Jemma hadn't minded—but she hadn't known it was with money that had been swindled out of the firm. A hollow laugh escaped her.

'There's no need to get upset, Jemma. Luke, here, has something to say to you—and it may be the perfect solution,' her father said placatingly.

'Just a minute,' Jemma snapped, shooting Luke a poisonous glance. 'This has nothing to do with you. You shouldn't even be here.'

'It's lucky for you I am,' he drawled sardonically, an unholy gleam of what looked to Jemma suspiciously like triumph lurking in the depths of his grey eyes. 'Unless, of course, you want your father to end up in jail for fraud.'

'Jail!' She turned stunned eyes on her father, fully expecting him to deny Luke's outrageous comment. 'Tell me that's not possible,' she pleaded.

'I'm sorry,' her father murmured, and got to his feet. His shoulders were slumped, his eyes dim, his face pale and worn; he was no longer the blue-eyed dynamic man she loved, but a weary old man who looked every one of his sixty years plus a decade more. She knew Luke was telling the truth. Her father reached down and put his hand on her shoulder, and she covered it compassionately with her own.

'I never meant this to happen, Jemma,' he said tiredly.

'If you don't mind I won't go to lunch with you. Take Luke instead; he will explain much better than I can what has happened. There might be a way out for us all if you and Luke can agree. God, I hope so. Because I dread telling Leanne what's happened if you can't.' Patting her on the head, he added, 'I'll see you tonight at the party.'

Suddenly the enormity of the situation finally sank into her brain. Her father being jailed for fraud was a real possibility, and he wanted her agreement to stop it happening. It didn't make sense. And why it was all right to involve *her*, when he dared not tell his wife, rankled more than a little. She needed answers from her father, who was heading for the door with some haste.

She got to her feet to follow him, but a strong hand snaked around her wrist and brought her to a stop with a jolt. Amazingly, for a few minutes she had forgotten Luke was present, but with his fingers warm against her skin, sending a tingling sensation up the length of her arm, she was forcibly reminded.

'Your father is some piece of work,' he stated cynically, and rose to his feet, dropping her wrist and slipping a restraining arm around her waist instead.

'No one asked for your opinion,' Jemma snapped, and tried to pull free. 'Let me go!' She glanced angrily up at him as he tightened his grip on her.

'So you can run after your father and interrogate him with questions he is in no fit state to answer?' he drawled, with a sardonic arch of one dark brow. 'I don't think so.'

'What the hell has it got to do with you?' Jemma cried. She had had enough; she was angry and confused, and the quicker she could get away from Luke's domineering presence the better.

'As a shareholder in Vanity Flair—everything, Jemma,'

he mockingly informed her, a wolfish smile that was no smile at all curving his firm lips.

Jemma had been so busy thinking of her father's dire situation she had given no thought to the shareholders involved, but now she did and exclaimed, 'Oh, my God! Your grandfather must have lost a fortune!'

'Don't worry about Theo, he's lost nothing. I bought his shares from him two months ago, so it's me you have to worry about. You heard your father: take me to lunch and all will be revealed.'

Jemma eyes widened as the full import of his words sank into her shocked mind. 'You... Then this is all your fault!' she burst out.

'No. It was your father's contemptible choice to steal in the first place,' Luke pointed out. But he saw the strained expression on her lovely face, the fear she could not quite hide in her extraordinary eyes, and he had the instinctive urge to protect her. Her father sure as hell hadn't. Jemma had no idea of the depth of her father's betrayal, of that he was sure, and for an instant he doubted the course of action he intended to pursue.

'My father is not a thief—the only contemptible person around here is you,' Jemma lashed back. 'It would make much more sense if it was *you* being accused of thieving.' Shackled by the curve of his arm, with the muscular length of his thigh hard against her and the warmth of his big body enveloping her, she discovered the light silk suit she wore suddenly seemed to take on the consistency of wool as heat surged through her and she panicked. She twisted to try and escape him, but surprisingly she didn't need to try very hard as Luke let her go and took a step back.

Any doubts Luke had had vanished at her insults. He had taken more than enough from this woman. Implacable determination glittered in his eyes as they raked over her. Her glorious hair was knotted loosely on the top of her head, a few stray tendrils framing her face. Lower down, the lapels of the fitted jacket she was wearing revealed the creamy curves of her breasts, defined her narrow waist, and the straight skirt clung to the gentle curve of her hips to end a few inches above her knees. Damn it! He wanted her, and he was going to have her.

'I've never stolen in my life. But I'll forget you said that, Jemma, because I know this has been something of a shock for you.' She was looking at him as if he was something the cat had dragged in, but beneath it he could sense her confusion. 'If you want to save your father and his company from ruin, I suggest we go to lunch. I'm hungry, and I'm much more generous when my appetite has been appeased. But it is your choice…'

Choice… The word echoed hollowly in Jemma's mind. Luke's parting comment the last time she had seen him came back to haunt her. She had sensed the threat in his words at the time, and dismissed it as her overactive imagination, but, looking at him now, she knew she had been right to be apprehensive. Luke was watching her with a hard, challenging gleam in his eyes and her heart sank like a stone. What choice did she have? Her own father had told her to listen to Luke…

'I'm not hungry.' She wiped damp palms down her thighs. 'And I have no wish to sit in a public restaurant with you and discuss my family business where anyone can overhear the conversation. But I am prepared to listen to what you have to say, and here is as good as anywhere.' She moved to sit down, not sure how long her shaking legs would hold her.

Luke stepped forward, his dark features hard as he looped a long arm around her shoulders. She stiffened, every self-protective instinct she possessed telling her to escape now, while she had a chance, but the image of her father's haggard face stopped her.

'I understand your concern,' he taunted mockingly, his silver-grey eyes capturing hers mercilessly. 'But I am hungry, and I know a place where the food is excellent and privacy is assured. Shall we go?'

CHAPTER SIX

WHICH was why, half an hour later, Jemma was in Luke's apartment, seated on a black hide sofa, a glass of white wine in her hand, looking on in dismay as Luke placed an assortment of cartons on the coffee table and whipped off the lids. He had ordered on the carphone as they'd left Connaught Square, and it was only then she'd realised she had made another mistake.

'I hope you like Cantonese,' he said blandly, handing her a bowl and chopsticks. She took the bowl, too stunned to do anything else, and when he forked some rice and salt-and-pepper prawns into it she found herself eating a couple.

But, with her nerves on a knife-edge, she refused his every offer of more, and instead studied the apartment through the thick veil of her lashes, wondering how she had allowed herself to be tricked into coming here. And what an apartment—all stark black, white and steel. No curtains at the wall of glass that was the window. A sunken lounging area lined with black hide seating and a glass table. A state-of-the-art media system that was operated by a small computer fitted into the arm of one of the seats. With a couple of large modern sculptures in bronze strategically placed on the polished wood floor, an ebony cabinet and black lamps, and a massive LCD TV mounted on a white wall, the place lacked any colour, any traces of a home. It was the ultimate in bachelor pads.

But Jemma was not really surprised—Luke Devetzi was hardly the homely type. In fact when she had calmed down enough to think about what had happened she began to feel slightly better.

Last month she had been called to her aunt Mary's solicitor and told probate had been granted and she now officially owned thirty per cent of Vanity Flair and the villa on Zante. She had already telephoned the man on the island who looked after the house and arranged to visit the second weekend in September, to decide what alterations were needed.

Jemma lived quite comfortably on the profit from the florist shop, and she had money from Alan's life insurance that she intended using to expand Flower Power. It looked as if she'd never have any dividend from the shares she now owned in Vanity Flair, but, worthless or not, she was a major shareholder and that must be why her father had said he needed her agreement to Luke's rescue plan. Obviously Luke wanted to recoup the money he had lost by buying Theo's shares from him, but Jemma would have some say in whether the company was wound up.

'Some more wine?' Luke interrupted her thoughts by offering the bottle, and hastily she covered her glass with her hand. It was wine that had got her into trouble with Luke in the first place, and she wasn't going to make the same mistake twice.

'No, thanks. I think it's time we got down to business, don't you? After all, that is why I'm here.' She continued bravely, 'Correct me if I am wrong, but it appears that, as I'm a major shareholder, you need my agreement to any plan to wind up my father's company, and you also can't decide what happens to him without my approval.'

Luke relaxed back against the sofa, a hint of a smile playing around his mouth. 'You're not exactly wrong.' He paused deliberately. 'You *are* the major shareholder, and as such stand to lose the most, and lawfully nothing can be done without your agreement.' Jemma breathed a silent sigh of relief, but her relief was short-lived as Luke continued, 'Unfortunately for you, your father's problems go back a long way. According to my information, until you reached the age of eighteen your father was the trustee of the ten per cent share your mother left you. Then you became a partner, along with your aunt and your father, and for the next four years, until you sold your mother's shares back to your father, you were directly responsible for running the company, along with the other family members. Luckily you were not a shareholder at the time of your father's worse excesses and the flotation on AIM. But technically, though it is unlikely, you could be accused along with your father for the early fraud.'

'Me!' Jemma exclaimed. 'Are you mad? That's impossible; I never had anything to do with the business. The shares my mother left me I sold back to my dad to help pay for the house Alan and I bought when we married. I had never even attended a board meeting until this summer, and only then at my dad's insistence because I had inherited Aunt Mary's shares. Whoever told you different is lying.'

'Your father told me,' he said bluntly, rising from the sofa. 'He couldn't do anything else, because I've seen your signature on earlier documents. Fair enough, you were young, but surely when your father showed you the accounts and asked you to verify and sign them you at least checked them?'

Ashen-faced, she stared up at Luke, at last beginning to realise the enormity of the situation. 'I never read them—I thought I was simply signing as a witness.'

'For what it's worth, I believe you. But it doesn't alter the fact that the only way to stop the whole business collapsing and the full weight of the law falling on your father is a vast injection of money.'

'How much cash?' she asked dully, and he mentioned a figure she would have had trouble writing down, never mind finding. 'I can sell my house, and in time the villa in Greece, I suppose.' She blinked to hold back the threat of tears. That her own father had involved her in his crime ten years ago was too incredible to believe. But sadly she recognised Luke was telling the truth. The defeated, guilty expression on her father's face and his hasty exit, leaving her to Luke's mercy, spoke louder than words.

'A drop in the ocean—to coin an English phrase,' Luke mocked. Dropping down on the seat beside her and cupping her chin in his hand, he turned her face towards him. 'But I do have a solution; I'm prepared to invest all the money necessary to get your father out of this mess and make the company viable again, but I want something in return.'

'I'm sure my father will do anything you say,' Jemma murmured. 'Basically he is a good man, but, well, he has…'

'An expensive wife and lifestyle,' Luke finished for her cynically. 'But it's not your father I'm interested in—it's you, Jemma. I want to marry you.'

The man had taken leave of his senses, was her first thought, and then she saw the determined gleam in the cold depths of his eyes and wasn't so sure.

'We can announce our engagement at your father's birthday party tonight.'

His suggestion was so outrageous it snapped Jemma out of the fog of despondency that had threatened to consume her. Picturing Jan's face, she almost laughed out loud. 'Are you crazy?' she exclaimed. 'You're my sister's boyfriend, for heaven's sake.' And suddenly Jemma saw the perfect solution to the problem. 'She's the one you should be asking, not me. I'm sure she'll jump at the chance.'

'Jan is an old acquaintance, nothing more.' His hand tightened on her chin. 'I swear I have never known her in the biblical sense—as I have you.' His heavy-lidded eyes seared into hers, the sensual knowledge in the gleaming depths making heat rush to her cheeks. 'So there's no problem there.' His long fingers moved from her chin to stroke up her cheek and curve a fine tendril of hair behind her ear, and inwardly she trembled as he added, 'Forget about Jan. If you want to save your father, marry me.' His deep, dark voice grated over her raw nerves, and her tongue flicked out to moisten her suddenly too-dry lips. She saw the knowing glint in his eyes at her betraying movement. 'It's your choice, and I want your decision now.'

It was that word *choice* again, and this time she was in no doubt that the threat was genuine. She jerked her head from his hold and leapt to her feet. 'But why me?' Jemma demanded, staring down at him. He was lounging back against the seat again, totally at ease, while she was standing on trembling legs wondering how a day that had started out so perfectly had turned into such a nightmare.

'Do you really need to ask?' Luke drawled mockingly, his masculine gaze roaming over her to linger on the lush curve of her breasts before reaching her face. 'You've been married before, Jemma, you're not that naïve.'

'Exactly,' Jemma jumped in. 'And I know what marriage is all about. Love is an integral part, and we don't love each other.' She didn't even like him! He was just too powerful, too arrogant, too wealthy, and just too domineering for Jemma. But at least she retained enough common sense not to insult him further by telling him so.

'Love doesn't exist—it's just another four-letter word

for lust,' Luke said cynically. 'And it has absolutely nothing to do with my proposal. To spell it out for you, I will personally make good the debts of Vanity Flair, buy out the smaller shareholders, take the company out of AIM, and turn it back into a family firm in which shares can only be exchanged between family members. One of my own men will be put in charge to make sure that your father, while retaining his position, won't be able to rob the company again. Obviously in return for the cash I need some surety, and that's where you come in. Marrying you makes me legally part of the family. Otherwise, there's no deal.'

Jemma swallowed the lump of fear that rose in her throat. 'But that's tantamount to blackmail...' she whispered. She shook her head to try and clear her thoughts, her eyes searching his face, looking for some sign that it was all a terrible joke.

But Luke's austere features were expressionless; he might as well have been conducting a board meeting. And in a way she supposed he was. Except that this time he was buying a marriage—and for a man who'd made his fortune trading on any commodity, why would this be any different? she thought bitterly.

'I still don't see what you get out of all this—other than a reluctant wife,' she said flatly. 'Then again, I could agree, and then divorce you six months later; that would leave me a heck of a lot richer and you even more out of pocket.'

'Nice try, Jemma.' He had the gall to grin as he rose to his feet and reached for her, his hands curving possessively around her shoulders. 'Sorry to disappoint you, but it's not quite that simple—there is one other condition. I want you to be the mother of my child, and to make sure of your compliance, my money will be fed into the company over the next three years.'

Mother of his child. Four simple words, but to Jemma very evocative. Her happiest childhood memories of her mother were when they had worked in the garden together, growing and nurturing plants and flowers. It was an intrinsic part of her nature to appreciate the continuity of life in all its forms. And for a moment the thought of having Luke's child stirred a basic response inside her. From the day she had married Jemma had always wanted a baby, but Alan had wanted to wait, and then it had been too late.

'So what's it to be, Jemma? Yes or no?' Luke asked, one hand moving from her shoulder to clasp the nape of her neck and tilt her face up to his. 'You know we're good together.' His dark head lowered—he was going to kiss her.

'No. No...' She pushed at his chest and hastily stepped back, putting some space between them. For a minute she had almost been seduced by his suggestion, and by the shameful need to feel his mouth on hers, to taste again the passion of his kiss, and yet Luke was trying to force her into marriage! Was she going mad?

'Pity.' Luke shrugged his broad shoulders. 'Two old men are going to be very disappointed—your father more than Theo, I fear.'

In a blinding flash of clarity Jemma saw it all. 'My God, that's it!' she cried, her golden eyes blazing angrily into his. 'I thought your grandfather was such a lovely old man, and yet between you you must have decided to ruin my father simply to get the house in Zante—or at least make sure your child did. I can easily believe that *you* are that devious, but I would never have thought it of Theo,' she accused bitterly. 'What is it with you Devetzi men? Is it your mission in life to destroy mine?'

'No,' Luke said harshly, his strong hand closing over her shoulders again. 'Theo has nothing to do with this. And whatever happens he is never to find out we had this conversation. He informed me after the party that he had given up on buying the villa because he had met you again and realised that you were a lovely woman who was unlikely to remain single or childless for much longer. So don't let what's happened between us spoil your opinion of Theo.'

'You really do care for him,' Jemma murmured, shocked; she hadn't thought Luke Devetzi capable of caring for anyone.

'Yes, of course I do.' His dark brows drew together in a brooding frown. 'I'm not totally devoid of human feeling, as you seem to think. But, to be brutally honest, marriage isn't something I've ever contemplated; the main reason I'm doing so now is because you told Theo that only your children can inherit the house on Zante. If I can please Theo and give him peace of mind by giving him the great-grandchild he longs for—a great-grandchild who will eventually inherit his old home—then that is worth any amount of money to me.'

For the first time since meeting Luke Jemma caught a glimpse of the man within, and she had a grudging respect for him. 'Is Theo your only family?' she asked.

'Yes, and as you have said no to my proposal he's likely to remain so, but for how much longer I have no idea.' Luke's hands fell from her shoulders and he gestured, palms up. 'He is an old man, after all.'

Though she didn't want to admit she had anything in common with Luke, she knew how he felt. Her father was her only blood relative left. 'If I don't marry you, what

will really happen to my father?' Jemma picked her words
with care, the kernel of an idea forming in her mind. She
had always wanted a child, and in her darker moments
since Alan's death she had thought her chance was gone.

'Once the story breaks, which it's bound to do without
any assistance from me because there are other shareholders, the worst-case scenario is that he will end up in
jail. The best that he can hope for is that he will end up
penniless.'

'And if I agreed, but with a few conditions of my
own…?' Jemma knew she would never fall in love again,
and although she had considered IVF in order to conceive
a child she wasn't entirely happy with the idea. But now
it appeared as though she had another choice—there was
that word again!—not a perfect choice, by any means, but
maybe it just might work.

'You're not really in a position to set any conditions,
but I am listening.'

Did she really want to do this? Jemma wasn't entirely
sure. For a moment she studied his implacable face. A
muscle tensed along his jaw and she could sense a latent
anger beneath the surface of his otherwise expressionless
face. As he could have his pick of women, she hadn't
been able to understand why he wanted her until he had
mentioned the house in Zante. But now she intuitively
recognised he had yet another reason. A man of Luke's
ego could not stand rejection. She had rejected him
twice..once after the night on the yacht and again two
months ago—and he had not forgotten. Somehow knowing that made it easier for her to continue, because she
knew he would soon have his fill of her and move on to
another woman, and hopefully she would be left with a
baby to love.

'I understand you travel a great deal with your work,

and spend a lot of time in America and the Far East. That wouldn't suit me at all. I would want a guarantee that I can continue to live in London and continue to run my own business.'

Luke gazed down at her with an enigmatic gleam in his grey eyes. 'Agree to marry me and I'll accept your conditions, with a couple of provisos.' He wondered if she had any idea she was offering him the best of both worlds—a wife to bear his child in London, and the freedom to pursue the lifestyle he enjoyed. 'We live here in my apartment and you sell your house. No other men in your life, obviously, and I would expect you to stay with me when I am at home in Greece with Theo. As for the rest—as you say, my work takes me all over the world. I see no necessity for you to travel with me, and certainly not when you have our child.'

To Jemma there was something very seductive about the words *our child*. If she married Luke, she would not really be betraying the love she had for Alan, she told herself, because there would be no love involved in her relationship with Luke. Just a straightforward bargain to save her father and give her the child she longed for.

'Jemma, is that a yes or a no? Do we have a deal?' Luke asked, and, tilting her chin with one long finger, he added, 'You know it makes sense.' His voice was suddenly velvety deep, and dark in its intensity. 'Marry me and be the mother of my child.'

Her stomach knotted with tension. His finger on her chin seemed to burn like a branding iron, and she hesitated. Luke had told her once that sometimes one had to choose between the lesser of two evils, and she knew now he was right. What was worse? A daughter refusing to marry a man she didn't love and condemning her father to jail? Or a daughter marrying a man she did not love to save her father and also to create a child to love? Neither was particularly laudable, but on balance the latter seemed the lesser of two evils.

'Yes,' she finally agreed.

'Good.' Luke's hand fell from her face and he gestured at the cluttered table. 'Then let's get this cleared up. We have an engagement ring to choose before tonight.'

'We do?' And the enormity of what she had agreed hit her like a punch in the stomach. Instinctively she glanced down and clasped her hands together, turning her gold wedding band around her finger. 'Is an engagement ring really necessary?' she murmured. It had never occurred to her that she would have to remove Alan's ring, and she wanted to delay the moment for as long as possible.

'Very necessary,' Luke said curtly, his hands closing around her upper arms. 'The whole point of an engagement ring is to declare that the woman is taken. Your husband has been dead for two years and you've lived in denial for long enough. Remove his ring before tonight; you don't need it any more.' Jemma tried to pull away, but Luke's fingers tightened. 'Face it, Jemma darling, I am your future,' he murmured, and he drew her inexorably closer into the heat and power of his tall frame.

Tension sizzled in the air. Angry and sad at the same time, Jemma saw the triumph in his wolf-like eyes and wanted to hit him. But before she could turn thought to action his dark head swooped and his mouth covered hers in a hard, demanding kiss. His tongue sought entry into the moist interior of her mouth, and when he finally lifted his head Jemma was sagging against him and fighting to breathe.

'Sealed with a kiss,' Luke mocked. 'Pity we haven't got time for more.' He grinned, his arms falling from her.

'But the jeweller awaits, and we have to get rid of this mess.'

Still reeling from the kiss, Jemma watched numbly as Luke turned and began to clear away with brisk efficiency. A less lover-like fiancée would be hard to imagine—but then theirs was no love-match, she reminded herself. Luke was a stockbroker and he had brokered a deal on marriage. Nothing more. She bent down to help clear the table, and, picking up the chopsticks, she had a strong urge to stab him in the back with one…

Jemma had thought Jan's birthday party horrendous, but it was nothing to the nightmare her father's birthday party was fast becoming. She was a teeming mass of quivering nerves and Luke's hand, which had rarely left her waist all evening, hadn't helped.

It was all Luke's fault. She should have realised when he'd swept her off to Bulgari's on New Bond Street that he actually meant what he'd said. He had paid a fortune for an impressive diamond and emerald ring, then driven her straight home and informed her he had some business to attend to but he would be back to pick her up at seven-thirty.

She had spent the rest of the afternoon wandering around her house in something of a daze. She had showered and dressed mechanically. It had only been when she'd slowly removed her wedding band that the full import of what she was doing had hit her. Her heart had filled with sadness and regret and she'd given way to a few tears.

But at seven-thirty Jemma had opened the door to him, wearing the classic black designer dress she had worn for Jan's party. She'd seen the flash of disapproval in his eyes, and then stiffened as he grasped her hand and carefully noted the pale line where her wedding ring had been. He'd given her a satisfied smile. 'Good girl, Jemma. But remind me to buy you some more colourful clothes. After all, the grieving widow is no more.' He'd led her to a waiting limousine, where a chauffeur had held the door open, and she'd slipped into the back seat, quickly followed by Luke.

Ignoring his crack about her widowed state, she asked, 'Why are we travelling in such style?' casting him a sidelong glance and trying not to think how handsome he looked in his immaculate evening suit.

'I always do when I intend to have a drink.' He reached into the inside pocket of his jacket for the stunning engagement ring and slipped it on her finger. 'I would imagine that a public celebration of our betrothal, plus the occasion of your father's birthday, will involve the drinking of numerous toasts and copious amounts of champagne.'

Jemma touched the beautiful emerald ring on her finger. 'Is this really necessary?' Glittering silver eyes locked with hers, and fear feathered down her spine. What had she done, agreeing to marry Luke? 'What will people think? My father and Leanne and their friends are never going to believe in a whirlwind wedding—not to mention Jan!'

'Yes, they will. Because I spoke to your father an hour ago. And, yes, the engagement ring is necessary—as the first prop, the traditions that surround a marriage. You and I know it's a business deal, but to the world at large it will appear as a conventional marriage—as long as you follow my lead and say nothing.'

Glancing once more at the sparkling jewel, she remembered the last time a man had put a ring on her finger—with love. Now it seemed to mock everything she had once believed in and she wanted to rip it off.

'Don't even think about it,' Luke growled, accurately

reading her mind, and before she could respond he was kissing her senseless.

It only got worse when they arrived at Connaught Square. Her father congratulated her, saying, 'Thank God you two have resolved your differences.'

Jemma was still trying to figure out what her father meant when Leanne, in a surprising show of affection, hugged her and wished her happiness. Jan was the biggest shock of all; with a very young and very handsome male model in tow, she also hugged Jemma and whispered in her ear, 'Well done, kid.'

That her family were happy for her was obvious. In fact, glancing around the crowd now, as far as Jemma could see everyone was happy except her. Without thinking she reached for the diamond studded locket around her neck. Stroking it between her fingers she relaxed a little, a soft sigh escaping her.

Luke felt her relax beneath his palm and thought it was because she was finally adjusting to the situation. He glanced down at her, a smile forming on his firm lips. But then he heard her sigh and saw she was idly playing with the locket around her neck, a faraway look on her beautiful face. She couldn't make it more obvious if she tried that she was bored.

His hand exerted pressure on her waist and subtly moved her in front of him, his eyes darkening with outrage. He wasn't used to the women in his life being anything other than totally absorbed with him, but Jemma had the ability to drift off into a world of her own and it infuriated him. 'Enjoying the party, darling?' he murmured silkily.

Jemma glanced warily up at him, but she refused to lie. 'No, I'm not really a party person—and especially not when I am the cynosure of all eyes because of your ring on my finger,' she said bluntly. It had been a devil of a day, and a pig of a night, and she could feel a headache coming on. She was fed up and had had enough.

'In fact, I'm going to find my father; I want a word with him. After all, this is supposed to be his birthday party, and you've rather hijacked the event. You can do what you like, but after I have spoken to Dad, I am going home,' she said defiantly, and, grasping his hand, she tried to remove it from her waist.

Luke could easily have restrained her, but, banking down his anger, he agreed. 'You're right. The engagement is now public, and we've been here long enough.' Dipping his head, he pressed a swift kiss on her softly parted lips and let her go. He was rewarded with a faint blush that coloured her pale face, and the sudden gleam of awareness in her incredible eyes. 'I'll give you ten minutes and then I'll come looking for you,' he promised, and he watched her spin around and edge through the crowd towards her father as if all the devils in hell were after her.

He smiled a wicked smile. For a woman who had been married she was remarkably naïve. Surely she realised that the pleasure of getting her alone far outweighed any desire Luke had to stay at the party. His blood heated at just the prospect of the night ahead.

As for Jemma, she could do nothing about the embarrassing colour in her cheeks. But as she saw her father slip out into the hall a light of challenge glittered in her eyes. Her dad was not getting away so easily. She wanted to hear the truth from his own mouth. Had he been aware of exactly what Luke had in mind from the beginning? And what had he meant by his comment that she and Luke had resolved their differences?

She reached the hall just time to see him disappear into his study, but before she could follow him a slightly inebriated Jan strolled up to her. 'You dark horse, Jemma. I've got to hand it to you—I would never have guessed.

Even when Luke took me to lunch after my birthday, told me he only considered me as a friend, and quizzed me about you, it never entered my head you knew him so well. Until…'

'Knew him so well!' Jemma exclaimed, the heat in her face draining away to leave her white as a sheet. Luke must have told Jan about their one-night stand, as he had threatened. How could he have been so cruel?

'You can drop the grieving widow look, Jemma. My mother told me all about you and Luke when I arrived this evening.'

'*Leanne* told you?' It was getting worse by the second, and Jemma didn't notice the reappearance of her father until he was beside her.

Beaming from ear to ear, he threw a paternal arm around her shoulder and hugged her. 'It's all right, Jemma, there's no need to look so shocked. You know Luke insisted I had to tell Leanne the truth about the company, and she was a bit upset at first. But when I told her you and Luke had known each other for over a year and had parted over a silly argument, and that he now wanted to try and resolve your differences and hopefully marry you, Leanne wanted to call you straight away—but I wouldn't let her.' Jemma glanced up and saw the proud expression on his face with incredulity. 'I said no, we were not to interfere, even though as my future son-in-law he had offered to save the business. And see how right I was? One lunch was all it took for you two to decide to make up, and I couldn't be happier.'

Or more relieved, she thought bitterly. 'Luke actually told you we knew each other?' she demanded.

'Don't look so surprised, Jemma; you must have known he was still keen at my party,' Jan said bluntly. 'And you might have told me you'd already met him in Greece and spent time on his yacht, instead of letting me make a fool of myself trying to get him into bed. But, hey! No hard feelings—the next best thing to a wealthy husband is a fantastically rich brother-in-law. I should have guessed when he offered to invest in my business while insisting we were just friends.'

Jemma's mouth worked but no sound came out. What was there to say? It was game, set and match to Luke. He came out of this as the generous, pining lover... What a joke! But she wasn't laughing. For a mad moment she was tempted to blurt out the truth—only after one look at their smiling, relieved faces she bit her tongue.

'Is this a private party or can anyone join in?' Leanne sauntered up and linked her arm through her husband's, smiling broadly at Jemma. 'I always knew there was more to you than met the eye, Jemma darling. Well done.'

Well done! She felt as if she had been turned over and spit-roasted, and white-hot rage consumed her. 'Thank you.' Not trusting herself to stay a second longer without exploding in fury at the injustice of the situation, Jemma turned to walk away and bumped straight into Luke. One long arm closed around her waist to steady her. She looked up and saw the glitter of mockery in his grey eyes and wanted to rip his throat out.

Knowing perfectly well she was furious, Luke hauled her hard into his side, the warning explicit in the firm touch of his fingers. He smiled at her father. 'You will excuse us? After all, this is your party, David.' Glancing down at Jemma he added, 'I think we've stolen enough of your father's thunder for one night, darling.'

Was it only she who noticed his emphasis on the word *stolen*? It was a seething but subdued Jemma who remained silent as Luke said goodnight to the other three...

CHAPTER SEVEN

THE moment she stepped out of the house Jemma turned to Luke. 'You bastard! How dare you—?'

'Save it, Jemma, and get in the car,' Luke said curtly. With his hand at her back he almost pushed her in and slid in beside her, throwing a long arm around her shoulders to hold her firmly in the seat. The car moved off after a brief command from Luke.

'Don't you order me around,' she snapped, her amber eyes clashing angrily with steel-grey. 'And how could you tell my father we were—' She stopped. Were what? Lovers? She couldn't say the word, and she hated the way he arched a sardonic black brow at her obvious reluctance to continue.

'Poor Jemma,' he taunted softly. 'You've buried your head in the sand for so long that when the truth is out you still can't admit the fact.'

'You wouldn't know the truth if it jumped up and bit you,' she spat. 'You're a devious, conniving swine, and you might be able to fool my father but you don't fool me.' She tore her gaze from his and shook her head. 'I must have been mad to think this arrangement would work.'

She felt his fingers dig into her shoulder as his free hand tilted her head back slightly, so she was forced to meet his eyes, and the look she saw in his glittering gaze made her tremble inside.

'No, you only fool yourself, Jemma. I do not lie—and I would kill a man for insulting me as you have,' he hissed

with sibilant softness, his nostrils flaring and his lips tightening into a hard bitter line. It struck her forcibly that
invoking his anger hadn't exactly been wise.

Luke in a fury was an impressive specimen of primitive
male. Inexplicably Jemma's heart stopped beating, and
she was aware of him as never before—the rise and fall
of his muscled chest beneath the conservative clothing,
the strong tanned column of his throat and the small pulse
that beat in his cheek. Her heart jerked back into a frantic
rhythm, and as she watched his handsome face was suddenly wiped clear of all expression. 'So consider yourself
lucky that I'm a man of restraint.'

'If you say so.' He didn't look very restrained to
Jemma, or feel it as his body leaned over hers, making
her nerves jangle with a host of sensations that were nothing to do with fear. She lost any desire to argue with him
as desire of a different kind brought a humiliating blush
to her cheeks.

'I do say so. And if this marriage is to have any chance
of convincing my grandfather and the world at large that
it is genuine, I suggest you start trying to do the same.
We have to present a united front—which shouldn't be
too difficult.' His face was only inches from hers, and his
hand slipped lower to curve around her breast, his thumb
apparently idly stroking the swelling peak through the fabric of her gown. 'And, with that in mind, I told your father
that we met a year ago and you visited me on my yacht.
We had a fight. The truth as far as it goes, you must
agree,' he murmured softly, his narrowed gaze dropping
to her mouth.

Heat coursed through Jemma's body and she lifted her
hand, intending to grasp his wrist, wanting him to desist,
but aching for more, but somehow her hand landed feebly
on his shirtfront, and she couldn't deny what he said was

true. 'Yes,' she whispered. He completely confused her, and his hand caressing her breast didn't help her thought processes one jot.

'So we are in agreement at last,' he said huskily, before adding, 'As for the rest, your father heard what he wanted to hear. And our appearance tonight as an engaged couple freed him of all guilt.' His head moved a fraction and his lips brushed across her mouth and back again, to harden and deepen into a long, possessive kiss. By the time he lifted his head, to Jemma's chagrin she was leaning against him, breathless and melting.

'I did you a favour, really, Jemma. Your family are convinced this is a love-match and can sleep happily in their beds free of any financial worry.' He gave her a knowing smile, his hand dropping from her breast to land casually on her thigh. She made a weak attempt to knock his hand away, but inside she was a quivering mass of electric excitement. 'And you can sleep happily in *my* bed, Jemma. You want me almost as much as I want you— though I don't expect you to admit it. But you will eventually. That I can promise you. In the meantime, as my soon-to-be wife and hopefully mother of my child, I expect you to behave as the sensible, sophisticated lady I know you to be—understood?'

Jemma silently nodded her head in agreement, not trusting herself to speak. Though she hated to admit as much, she understood perfectly. Luke's version of events saved face all round—hers included.

He was helping her out of the car before she had fully realised it had stopped. 'Wait,' she protested, glancing around. 'This isn't my street.'

'No, it's mine. You and I have a lot to discuss; I'm leaving for New York tomorrow. The details of our wedding must be decided before I go, and I have no intention of doing that in the home you shared with your late husband.'

About to refuse, she stopped. Financially he held all the cards, and physically, for some unknown reason, just the sight of him was enough to send her pulse racing—and he had done a damn sight more than look at her in the car, as her wayward body was hotly reminding her. 'Okay.'

'Very wise,' he taunted softly, slipping a hand around her elbow and ushering her into the foyer. He stopped at the security desk and introduced her to the uniformed attendant. 'Sam, this is Jemma—my fiancée. I'm leaving tomorrow, but Jemma will be moving in here next week, so I'd appreciate it if you would accord her every courtesy, and inform the rest of your crew.'

'Was that really necessary?' Jemma demanded as soon as the elevator doors swung closed behind them. 'I mean—'

'You mean what? You would prefer to wait until after we are married to move in? Grow up, Jemma. You're an experienced woman of twenty-eight and you know the score as well as I do, so no more pretence. We have a deal, and the sooner you accept the fact, the better it will be for both of us.'

The experienced woman bit was rather flattering; the rest she wasn't so sure about, and when he placed a hand at her back and urged her into the massive lounge of his apartment she had the childish desire to turn and run. But, sensing her ambivalence, Luke stroked his hand up her spine and settled around her shoulders. A minute later she was seated on the black sofa, watching as Luke strolled over to the drinks cabinet, removing his jacket and tie as he did so and dropping them on a seat.

He glanced back over his shoulder. 'Would you like a drink?'

'Just mineral water, please. Two glasses of wine is my limit.' She saw his grimace as he turned back to the cabinet, but a moment later he returned with two crystal glasses and handed her one.

'Water, as requested,' he said sardonically, and casually lowered his long length down beside her. 'We really do need to talk, Jemma. I made some enquiries earlier, and it takes about sixteen days to marry in England. As you've already had a big wedding with your family, I thought we'd have a simple civil ceremony two weeks on Saturday. After I left you this afternoon, I gave notice to the registrar's office. It only remains for you to call in with your papers. How does that sound?'

Terrifying! This was supposed to be a discussion? What a joke—Luke already had everything cut and dried, as far as she could see. Except she had plans of her own, and she wasn't going to allow him to ride roughshod over them. But, mindful of his comment about her age and sophistication, Jemma forced herself to reply coolly. 'That won't be possible, I'm afraid, because I won't be here. I've already arranged with Liz to take two weeks off before that. I have my flight booked for a week on Saturday; I'm going to Zante to meet with the man who takes care of my aunt's house and decide what repairs and decorating need doing. The wedding will have to be later, when I get back.'

'Rubbish.' Luke turned towards her. His white dress shirt was open at the neck and gave her a disturbing glimpse of tanned flesh and black chest hair which she could have done without. She was just beginning to get her breath back from the episode in the car. Swallowing hard, she tried to concentrate on what he was saying. 'It couldn't be more perfect. I can easily arrange for us to marry in Greece.'

'In Greece?' Jemma parroted incredulously.

'It's the ideal solution. We can be married a week on Saturday at my home. I'll arrange for your family and friends to fly out, and Theo will be spared the hazard of travelling. We can honeymoon on Zante for the first week, to sort out the house, then go somewhere else. Theo can take over and supervise the alterations.'

'No, we can't stay in the house,' she contradicted him flatly. 'And neither can Theo—the place isn't fit for him to live in.'

'Okay, we can stay in a hotel, and Theo will have to wait to see his old home.' His grey eyes gleamed with mocking amusement as he added, 'But it is about time I saw the house that's costing me a fortune and my freedom.'

'You've never seen the house?' Jemma queried. 'But I naturally assumed you were born there.'

'No, Theo was born there, and so was my mother.' Luke drained his glass and placed it on the table, the slight smile vanishing from his handsome face to be replaced with a frown. 'But I was born in Athens, and my mother wasn't married. So you see I am the bastard you called me.'

A blush suffused her face at the reminder of her earlier outburst. If she had known he was illegitimate she would never have been so tactless. She opened her mouth to apologise, but Luke briefly laid a silencing finger across her lips.

'Don't bother, I don't mind, but unfortunately my grandmother did. So she insisted that Theo sell up and they all moved to Athens, where no one knew them. My mother died a few days after I was born, and my grandparents brought me up. Theo mentioned Zante once or twice, but my grandmother never did, and I had no interest in the place. In fact, and it shames me to admit it, I never realised Theo was that bothered about it until I discovered that ever since my grandmother died he's been trying to buy the place back.'

'But why didn't he try sooner?' Jemma asked.

A broad grin spread across Luke's handsome face, making him look almost boyish. 'Theo didn't dare, and I don't blame him. If you'd ever met my grandmother you'd know why—she was a small, lovable, but extremely formidable lady. She decreed that they would never look back or so much as mention Zante again when they left the island. She was also as stubborn as a mule, and it would have taken a braver man than Theo or I to defy her.'

He can really be quite human, Jemma thought, trying to imagine the little Greek lady who had had the power to intimidate Luke Devetzi. 'I would have loved to meet her,' Jemma said wryly. 'And learn her secret,' she added, her lips curving back over her even white teeth in a mischievous smile.

It was the first real smile she had given him, and Luke drew in a sharp breath. He reached out and cupped her head in his palms, his gaze dropping to her sweetly parted lips. 'I have a sneaking suspicion you might already know it,' he husked, and gently covered her tempting mouth with his own. He felt her slight resistance, and then the warmth of her breath mingled with his, and with the slightest touch of her tongue all thought of gentleness faded.

He deepened the kiss with a probing, hungry passion, exploring the moist interior of her mouth as he ached to explore the tight, moist interior of her incredible body that he remembered so well. He felt her arms reach up and stifled a groan at the softness of her fingers on the nape of his neck.

Easing the zip of her dress down her back, he raised his head to stare down at her, his hands deftly sweeping the dress from her shoulders to her waist. He had Jemma exactly where he wanted her, and he battled to control the urge to take her here and now, on the sofa. Her incredible golden eyes were dazed with desire, and her lush breasts were firm and full, with exquisite rose-pink nipples that were begging to be tasted.

'Are you going to make me wait until the wedding, Jemma?' he rasped, and then cursed himself for being fifty kinds of a fool. A wonderful willing woman in his arms and he had to stop and ask. 'Are you on the pill?' he asked, in a poor attempt to justify his idiocy.

For Jemma it had been like diving off a cliff into uncharted seas. Every nerve in her body quivered with sensual excitement and she ran her tongue over her kiss-swollen lips, savouring the taste of Luke. She was hazy as to how it had happened, but with her blood pulsing heavily through her veins she stared up at him. She saw the flush of colour across his high cheekbones, the barely leashed passion in the depths of his silver eyes, and without thinking she surrendered completely to the urgent dictates of her body. 'No to both questions.'

He swept her up in his arms, and she squealed, 'What are you doing?' as he pounded up the few steps to the main floor.

'Taking you to bed.' He laughed down into her startled eyes. 'What else?' And before she had time to catch her breath he was lowering her onto a huge bed. 'Where you were meant to be,' he said, a gleam of triumph in his silver gaze as his fingers dealt swiftly with his shirt.

The coolness of the cover on her back and the realisation that her dress was already half off had her blushing furiously and crossing her arms defensively across her chest. She heard his chuckle and glanced back up, her eyes widening in awed fascination at his bronzed near-naked body.

He was so magnificently male—wide-shouldered, with a broad, muscular chest that had a dusting of black body hair that arrowed down to disappear beneath the waistband of his black silk boxer shorts. Shorts that bulged to an alarming degree and had her blushing even more furiously. Her gaze dropped lower, to view his muscular thighs and long legs. God, what was happening to her? she groaned inwardly, tearing her eyes away from him before she did the unthinkable and lunged at him.

'No need to blush, Jemma.' She felt the mattress depress and the heat of his body against her side. Trembling, she glanced up to find Luke propped up on one elbow, his sensuous lips curved in a sexy smile. 'And no need to hide your exquisite body, either,' he husked, reaching for one of her hands and placing it on his shoulder. Her fingers flexed on his satin-smooth skin, and she shivered as he took her other hand and pressed it to the bed, revealing her naked breasts to his avid gaze.

'You have perfect breasts,' he murmured, his molten silver eyes meeting hers, and heat washed all through her. Then, dipping his head, he laved each straining nipple with his tongue, shooting needles of excitement from her breast to the apex of her thighs. Involuntarily she arched up towards him and he curled his hand into the folds of her dress, slipping the gown from her body. 'I want to see you naked,' he growled as her lace panties followed her dress. 'With your magnificent hair loose across my pillow.' And, suiting his actions to his words, he raked his fingers through her hair, dislodging the lightly pinned chignon, and pulled the long strands down across her shoulders and breasts.

Trembling with excitement, Jemma was past caring about her hair. Her golden gaze flicking to his mobile mouth, she drew in an unsteady breath, hungry for his kiss. She tightened her hand on his shoulder and tried to urge him closer. He knew what she wanted, and with a teasing smile briefly dipped his head and brushed his mouth against hers. She groaned her disappointment as he leant back again.

'Patience, Jemma, I want to examine every inch of you.' His hand curved around her throat and then trailed with tactile delight over her breast and the indentation of her waist. His glittering gaze swept down over her shapely length and back to her face. 'I want to taste every inch of you,' he amended shakily, his hand stroking lower, to her thigh. His head lowered and his lips, gentle as thistledown, trailed warm kisses over her brow, the tender skin of her eyelids, the soft curve of her cheek. 'Because this time I want there to be no doubt in your mind who's possessing you.'

A flicker of unease tugged at her consciousness, but it had been too long since she had been naked in a man's arms, since she had felt the fierce pleasure of sexual arousal, and she wanted Luke badly. She reached for him with both hands and felt every pore of her skin open with the heat of his hard naked body against her own. Her lips parted in anticipation of his kiss and he did not disappoint. His mouth covered hers, his tongue stroked the sensitive roof of her mouth and her own tongue duelled with his while her slender arms wrapped around his broad back, her fingers reaching up to tangle in the soft black hair of his head.

Luke's strong hand curved lovingly around a firm breast, his teasing fingers plucking at the sensitized, aching tip, and a low moan escaped her, her body on fire for him. His hand slid down over her stomach and she shuddered violently as his long fingers stroked through the soft curls at the junction of her thighs and found the hot liquid centre of her femininity. She whimpered with pleasure, her nails digging into his back, as he stroked the swollen nub of exquisite sensitivity until she was writhing beneath him, every nerve in her body taut with unbearable tension. Her hands moved down his back, and lower, to dig into the flesh of his thighs. She wanted to feel the full power of his possession and yet didn't want him to stop the feverish delight of his caressing fingers.

'Yes, open for me, Jemma,' Luke rasped, and once more he captured her swollen lips in a savage kiss as he moved to settle between her legs. The hard, rigid length of his arousal pressed against her inner thighs, but no further. She moaned deep in her throat, desperate for his ultimate possession. But he raised his head and she stared at him with wild eyes. 'Not yet.' His mouth curved in a purely male predatory smile. 'I want you to remember this for the rest of your life,' he growled.

Once more his head descended, his mouth capturing the engorged peak of one breast. His teeth bit lightly, and she jerked involuntarily, caught up in a game where only Luke knew the rules. She nipped at his shoulder, her hand sliding across his thigh, her fingers finding his hard shaft. But he tore her hand free and pinned it to the mattress with his own while he explored every inch of her with an erotic intimacy she had never thought possible, bringing her to the brink of pleasure over and over again. Then his mouth found hers, his tongue thrusting with an insinuating rhythm while his long fingers slid between her legs, sending shock waves crashing through her.

Jemma could stand it no longer. Pressing fierce kisses to his massive chest, she pleaded, 'Please, Luke.' Her teeth found a small male nipple and bit it in a frenzy of need.

Her plea ringing in his ears, Luke lifted her hips and drove into her incredibly tight silken sheath with a powerful thrust that brought a shuddering groan of sheer ecstasy from his throat. For the first time in twenty years he was making love without the use of protection, and he paused, fighting to control the intensity of sensation that exploded through every atom of his body.

'Luke!' Jemma cried out his name as she felt the pulsing strength of him stretch and fill her, and then slowly he withdrew. 'No, no—don't stop,' she moaned frantically.

'I couldn't if I tried,' Luke grated desperately, and began to drive into her again and again, taking her in a fierce primitive rhythm that Jemma met and matched, until seconds later her body convulsed in a shattering climax.

Jemma felt Luke's shuddering release as he collapsed on top of her, her inner muscles clenching spasmodically around him as his seed spilled inside her. She clung to him, her hands instinctively caressing his broad shoulders, stroking over the satin-smooth shoulderblades, her fingers tracing the indentation of his spine, awed by the power and the wonder of their coupling. The weight of his magnificent body pinned her to the bed, and the tortured sound of their breathing was the only sound in the stillness of the room.

Later, although how much later—one minute or ten—Jemma was incapable of knowing, Luke eased his now familiar weight off her, and leant on one forearm, looking intently into her beautiful, love-dazed face. 'That was amazing, Jemma,' he declared with a broad grin. 'And, in case you have any doubt, that was the first time since I was a teenager that I neglected to use protection. I can assure you I have a totally clean bill of health, so you have nothing to worry about.'

It was the smug masculine satisfaction in his tone that infuriated Jemma, and brought home as nothing else could how far apart they were in the sexual stakes. With the one exception of Luke, a year ago, she had only slept with Alan. But Luke was the direct opposite; he had had so many lovers that health checks were probably a necessity of life for him.

'Thank you for that,' she said, barely containing her sarcasm. 'But now, if you don't mind—' she edged away from him '—I have to get home. Friday is a busy day at work.' She slipped her feet over the side of the bed and stood up, terribly conscious of her nudity but determined not to show it. 'I have to be at the market by five a.m., and I would like to get a couple of hours' sleep first.' She moved to the foot of the bed and picked up her crumpled dress. She slid it over her head, *sans* underwear, before she dared to glance back at Luke.

He was sprawled across the bed, his head propped up on one hand, his black hair sexily dishevelled. 'Pity. Are you sure I can't tempt you back to bed?' he asked lazily. 'I don't have to leave for New York until nine.'

The devil of it was he *could* tempt her. In fact, he could probably tempt a saint, Jemma wryly conceded. 'No, remember our deal, Luke. I keep my career.'

'Okay.' He leapt up off the bed, gloriously naked and unfazed. 'But remember the rest of it, Jemma: you move in here before I return from New York.' And, grasping her chin, he planted a swift, hard kiss on her mouth. 'Give me five minutes and I'll take you back.'

Jemma noticed he didn't say 'back home', and for a fleeting instant she wondered if Luke could be jealous of her late husband and the life they had shared. No, that was impossible; that would imply Luke cared about her, and she knew for a fact that he didn't. She saw him disappear into bathroom and hastily scrabbled around to find her panties and her purse. When he returned, dressed in denim jeans and a sweater, she was fully clothed and trying to twist her tumbled mass of hair into some kind of order.

'Leave it—you're only going to bed,' Luke commanded.

He left her at her front door with a brief hard kiss. Twenty minutes later she crawled into bed, physically exhausted, but with her mind in turmoil. She didn't understand herself any more. Why had she let the thought of a baby propel her into an impulsive decision to marry Luke? Why had she let a man she didn't like and certainly didn't trust make love to her? She closed her eyes in bewilderment and shame. She didn't recognise herself. Because she hadn't simply let Luke make love to her, she had been a willing, even eager participant—as her aching body reminded her.

CHAPTER EIGHT

'DAMN!' Jemma cursed as she put down the phone, turning stormy eyes on Liz. 'That was Luke again. Would you believe it? Apparently I'm to take tomorrow off work because *he* has arranged for me to go clothes-shopping with Jan at his expense! The nerve of the man! Does he think I'm incapable of dressing myself?' She glared at the telephone in exasperation, and Liz burst out laughing.

'No, of course not. As a man, he probably thought it was a good way of mending any rift he may have caused between you and Jan because he dated her to get close to you and win you back. Luke's obviously crazy about you, and I think it's so romantic the way he phones you several times a day. If you had any sense you would take the rest of the week off as well, and pamper yourself ready for his return.'

Romantic, my foot, Jemma thought mutinously, but said nothing. Last Friday she had told Liz she was engaged and given her Luke's version of events. Surprisingly, Liz had swallowed the story whole, and was delighted for her. Now it was Tuesday, and Luke was due back from New York on Thursday. They were flying out to Greece with her family on Friday, for the wedding the following day. The only reason he kept calling her was to inform her of every minute detail of the wedding arrangements. As if she cared! The telephone rang again, and Jemma jumped.

'You answer it, Liz, and if that's Luke again tell him

109

I'm out,' she snapped. 'Tell him I've gone to move my stuff into his apartment.'

'And are you?' Liz asked, reaching for the phone.

'Yes, I am,' Jemma said. 'In fact, I'll take the rest of the week off, as you suggested—if you're sure you can manage?'

'Of course I can.'

'Great—I'll see you at the wedding on Saturday.' She slung her bag over her shoulder and dashed out of the shop before Liz could change her mind. If she heard one more comment from Liz, her father, Jan or anyone on how lucky she was to have landed a gorgeous multimillionaire, she would scream. Plus, she had an important visit to make that she could put off no longer.

After a quick stop at home to wash and change she drove down to Eastbourne. She wasn't looking forward to telling her in-laws she was marrying again, but surprisingly Sid and Mavis took the news remarkably well and were happy for her, telling her she was too young to stay single for the rest of her life and that Alan would have said the same.

Late the next afternoon, feeling hot and harassed, Jemma shoved the shoestring strap of the simple blue slip dress she was wearing back on her shoulder for about the tenth time, unlocked the door of her house and walked in. Shopping and lunch with Jan had been exhausting, and she dropped the bags she was carrying on the hall table, flexing her aching hands and looking at the emerald and diamond ring on her finger.

Nervously she twisted it round and round as she walked into the living room. Time was running out; Luke would be back tomorrow, and she hadn't even started to pack or organise her house sale. But did she really need to? A tiny rebellious imp in the back of her mind posed the question.

She wandered around, touching the familiar items. She picked up her wedding photo, a reminiscent smile curving her mouth, then put it back, her mind made up.

An hour later she locked the door behind her, leaving her home as it always had been, and drove across London to Luke's apartment with three cases in the boot of her car, packed with clothes and the essentials for everyday living.

Sam insisted on carrying her luggage up to the penthouse, and she smiled her thanks and gave him a large tip before closing the door behind him. Jemma glanced around the living room; it was as stark as she remembered. She checked out the state-of-the-art stainless steel kitchen. The dining room was much the same—just glass and steel.

The bedrooms were not a lot better—one white, one blue, functional but soulless. The only surprise was the study, comfy, with book-lined walls, an antique desk, tons of electronic equipment, of course, but also a very attractive fireplace and two high-backed winged armchairs covered in the softest mint-green hide.

She picked up a suitcase and entered the master bedroom. She hadn't taken much notice of the décor the last time she'd been here, and she was pleasantly surprised. The room was decorated in tones of cream and indigo, and a thick cream carpet with a Grecian border in indigo covered the floor. Long flowing drapes were held back with indigo ties to reveal large glass doors that opened onto a terrace at one side of which was a plump cushioned sofa, chair and a low table. The whole ambience was much softer than in the rest of the apartment.

Jemma's glance strayed to the massive bed in the centre of the room and an unexpected surge of heat coloured her skin. Quickly she looked away. On the opposite side of the room were two doors, and hastily she walked over.

She opened the first to discover a luxurious white bathroom, with a double shower and double vanity basins, and in the corner, raised on a dais, a huge whirlpool bath. She closed the door and tried the next one, finding it opened into a dressing room with fitted wardrobes and the same thick carpet following through.

Jemma quickly unpacked her suitcases and stowed her clothes away. There was plenty of free space; Luke's clothes barely filled one of the wardrobes. Obviously he didn't spend much time here, she thought as she placed her make-up box on the dressing table, and that was good...wasn't it? Lifting her jewellery box from the case, she missed the table and spilt the meagre contents on the floor.

On her hands and knees, with her head under the table, Jemma was still trying to find the last item of jewellery five minutes later—her platinum heart-shaped locket.

'Now, that is what I call a welcoming sight!' Luke's body responded with instant masculine enthusiasm on seeing the pert buttocks barely covered by blue silk stuck up in the air, and he chuckled. He recognised that rear with delight, and the relief he felt at finding Jemma already in his apartment was almost euphoric. Unable to resist, he patted her bottom.

Jemma heard the familiar voice a moment before she felt the hand pat her bottom. Her head jerked up and she hit it on the underside of the table. 'What the hell?' she screeched, and backed out from beneath the table, rolling onto her back and lifting stormy eyes to her nemesis. 'You almost knocked me out, you great baboon.' She lifted a hand to rub her head. To add insult to injury, the hateful man was laughing like a drain...

'I'm sorry,' Luke spluttered. Her glorious hair was in a tousled mass about her shoulders, her amber eyes as bright as topaz against her flushed skin. The blue silk dress was twisted around her shapely curves, revealing more of her rounded breasts than she was aware of, and his body tightened another notch. 'But you have a delightful backside, Jemma, and I couldn't resist.' He reached down a hand to help her to her feet.

Flustered by his unexpected appearance, and well aware of his amused male scrutiny, her heartbeat accelerated alarmingly. Ignoring his hand, Jemma scrambled inelegantly upright. 'Then it's about time you tried,' she snapped. 'You're a bit long in the tooth to be smacking a woman's bottom,' she said nastily.

'My, you *have* led a sheltered sex life, Jemma darling,' he drawled, with a mocking amusement that incensed her even more. Because over the last few days and restless nights, with the memory of his lovemaking fresh in her mind, she had had the same traitorous thought.

'No one can say that of you, that's for sure,' she shot back, her amber eyes meeting his, and she saw the amusement vanish to be replaced with a much more dangerous gleam. 'And what are you doing here?' She changed the subject abruptly. 'You weren't supposed to be back until tomorrow.'

'I finished earlier than I expected.' He stepped closer, and Jemma stepped back, but was stopped by the edge of the dressing table. 'I couldn't wait any longer.' His hands fastened on her waist and he smiled, a darkly sensual twist of his lips, then slid one hand up her spine to clasp the back of her head. 'To see you.' His dark head bent and Jemma's first instinct was to struggle. 'And do this,' he breathed against her mouth, his tongue slipping between her parted lips. With the warm, moist taste of his tongue against hers Jemma's heart leapt in her breast, and any thought of struggling was lost in the hungry pleasure of his mouth.

She melted against him, her hands of their own volition stroking across his shoulders. She was intoxicated by the scent of him, the enveloping power of his embrace, the driving passion of his mouth, and when he ended the kiss she groaned in protest.

Luke muttered something that was unintelligible and lifted her onto the table. His mouth covered the pulse that beat madly in her throat and sucked at the soft flesh with ferocious intensity, and when he slipped the strap of her dress from her shoulder and covered her breast her nipple peaked instantly against the palm of his hand.

His hand fell away, and she moaned out loud as his mouth enveloped the aching peak. With tongue and teeth he drove her wild. Then his hand found the hem of her skirt and slid up to stroke over the silk of her panties between her thighs. She gave a tortured gasp and he lifted his head. Their eyes met, the question asked and answered without a word being spoken, and his fingers slipped beneath her panties and caressed her damp silken flesh even as his mouth moved once more to torment her other breast.

Jemma had never experienced anything like it, so hot and instant was her arousal. She gasped, her legs instinctively parting to give him better access, her thighs quivering as she teetered on the brink of climax. Then suddenly he stopped and straightened, and only her elbows stopped her falling flat on the dressing table. His hand slid down her thigh and took her panties off with incredible ease.

She stared, wild-eyed and wanting, as she watched him unzip his fly. Then in a frenzy of explosive passion his hands slid under her to grasp her buttocks and he thrust into her, forcing her back with the driving power of his possession so that instinctively she locked her legs around his waist. His mouth crashed down on hers as he thrust to the hilt, again and again, each stroke of his rigid pulsating flesh driving her higher and higher until their bodies climaxed together in a volcanic explosion of fire and liquid heat. His hips jerked to a shuddering halt while Jemma clung to him with arms and legs as her inner muscles continued to convulse around him.

Luke cursed under his breath. He had never lost control and taken a woman so quickly since he was a callow youth, and the last thing he'd wanted was to frighten Jemma off days before the wedding. He saw the shock in her eyes, and, pushing the straps of her dress back over her shoulders, he withdrew from her body. Holding her steady with one hand, he quickly adjusted himself and zipped up his fly. Then he lifted her off the table and smoothed the dress down over her hips. 'Jemma…' He said her name and she looked at him with huge rounded eyes but didn't say a word. 'Are you okay?'

Jemma was too stunned to speak, and too embarrassed to hold his gaze. She felt as if she had been hit by a lightning bolt, whereas Luke was fully dressed and not even the knot in his tie had moved. An instant replay of the last five minutes flashed in her mind and she blushed fiery red. Perched on the table, with her dress around her waist, totally exposed, she had never felt such primitive lust in her life before. Her gaze finally lifted warily to Luke's face, to see him watching her with a guarded expression.

Was she okay? She lowered her eyes again—and it was the tie that did it. She laughed, and if there was a touch of hysteria in the sound Luke didn't appear to notice. 'I'm fine,' Jemma said when she could finally control her voice. 'And you were right earlier—I am a bit naïve about sex. I've never experienced sheer animal lust before,' she told him honestly. 'I suppose I could get used to it, in moderation, though I think I prefer a bed.'

'Is that an invitation?' Luke grinned, and, reaching out, he gently brushed a few stray tendrils of her hair behind her ear.

She heard slight relief in his tone, mingled with the blatant sexuality of suggestion. 'No,' she said swiftly, and attempted a sophisticated smile back.

Basically, Luke was a magnificent specimen of the male sex. He was extremely successful, and he had a very high sex drive that he indulged wherever and with any woman he wanted to. But then she had always known that, so it was no real surprise. What did surprise her was the knowledge that she was equally capable of enjoying sex without any emotional attachment to the person she was having sex with. Perhaps she was becoming the sophisticated woman Luke had called her. But now was not the time for self-analysis, with Luke watching her, so, blanking all thoughts of sex from her mind with some difficulty, Jemma straightened her shoulders and sidestepped away from him. 'Before you appeared,' she said, returning to what was really important to her, 'I was looking for something I had dropped on the floor.'

'So that's why you were under the table; I did wonder when I saw your bottom in the air.' He chuckled.

'Yes, well, my locket isn't under there.' Jemma frowned, not in the least amused, and glanced around the floor. 'It must have bounced off the table and got hidden in the carpet somewhere.' She looked at Luke. 'Be careful where you step because I don't want it broken; it was a present from Alan on my twenty-first birthday.'

Luke was taken aback by Jemma's revelation. Till now

he had been more than satisfied—Jemma responded to him sexually and had agreed to their marriage—but now he was far from satisfied. That she could switch from having such intense sex with him to thinking about her late husband two minutes later was not particularly flattering to his male ego.

'I'll help you look,' Luke offered, but the sad little smile and murmured thanks Jemma gave him in return infuriated him still further. His gimlet gaze sweeping around the floor, he quickly spotted the locket and casually moved to step on it. 'Oops, I appear to have found it.' He bent down and picked up the very much dented locket. 'Sorry about that, Jemma.' And he dropped the mangled locket in her outstretched hand. He wasn't proud of his actions, but anything was permissible in love and war. He stiffened. Love? Where the hell had that come from? Love was not a word in his vocabulary... 'I need to shower and change,' he said abruptly, tugging at his tie and feeling very hot under the collar. 'I'll buy you another locket.'

Jemma glanced down at the locket in her hand and curled her fist around it. It was her last link with Alan, she thought with a bittersweet sadness. Well, not quite the last link—she still had the house, and she refused to feel guilty about deceiving Luke. 'Thanks, but that won't be necessary,' she said coolly, lifting her head and looking straight at him, but he avoided her gaze.

'As you like.' His broad shoulders lifted in a shrug and Jemma had the oddest notion he had deliberately broken her locket. 'I'd like a coffee, but don't bother with anything to eat—I have a bit of work to do in the study. We can go out to dinner later on.' As she watched he removed his jacket, then started on his shirt buttons.

He infuriated her! She hadn't intended cooking for him

anyway. She opened her mouth to tell him as much, but then stopped. She hadn't really thought about the practicalities of living with Luke, but now she was forced to. In three days they would be husband and wife, and unless she wanted her life to become a living hell she had to ignore the reasons why he was marrying her and try to have a civilised relationship with him. She curled the locket in the palm of her hand... The end of an era...

'Okay, I'll get you that coffee,' she murmured. In her fragile state, Jemma didn't need to see him strip naked, and she darted out of the room to the kitchen.

Later, seated at an intimate table for two in an exclusive restaurant, lingering over a cup of coffee after an excellent meal, Jemma allowed herself a smile.

'What's amusing you?' Luke asked, taking a sip of brandy from a balloon glass.

'I was just thinking it's ironic that this is the same restaurant I was going to bring my father to for his birthday, and instead I got you. In a few days' time we'll be married, and yet this is the first time we have actually been out together. Doesn't it bother you that you know nothing about me, Luke?'

The meal had been wonderful, and to her surprise Jemma had discovered Luke was an intelligent and witty companion—when he wasn't trying to get her into bed.

'Not in the slightest.' He put down his glass and put his hand over hers resting on the table. 'I know all I need to know. You're a very beautiful and sexy woman.'

'I didn't mean sex.' She tried to pull her hand away, but his fingers linked with hers and prevented her.

'Let me finish. I know we are compatible in that area.' He freed her hand and, leaning forward, reached to tilt her chin with one finger, his silver eyes holding hers. 'There's a powerful chemistry between us—you can't deny it. You melt when I touch you, and it's the same for me. That's a big plus in any marriage.. and as for the rest, we have a lifetime to get to know each other.' Heat scorched Jemma's cheeks. The sexual tension was back in full force, and she heaved an inward sigh of relief when Luke sat back and was silent for a moment. Then he continued, 'But I also know you and I both want the same thing—to have a child or two and be a family, and at the same time make the families we already have happy.'

'And you think that's enough?'

'It's a lot more than most people in this day and age aspire to,' he said rather cynically. 'A growing percentage of people have a child with no more thought than they would give to buying a new coat, and they cast off their responsibilities with the same ease as shedding a coat.' He leant forward again. 'But let me reassure you, Jemma. Although I travel a great deal, once we have a child my schedule will be rearranged. I won't be an absent parent.'

Surprise at his comment kept her silent, not sure she wanted to be reassured about his possible increased presence in her life. He rose to his feet and dropped a bundle of notes on the table. 'Come on, let's go,' Luke instructed, and walked around to her side, and held out his hand to her. Jemma took it...

The next morning Jemma woke up in Luke's bed, muscles aching in places she'd never known she had. There was no sign of Luke, and, leaping out of bed, she shot into the shower. Thanking her lucky stars that she had brought some clothes over yesterday, even if it had been in a fit of temper, she pulled on a pair of oatmeal-coloured trousers and teamed them with a matching silk blouse. She brushed her hair and tied it back with multi-coloured scarf, slipping her feet into soft suede mules. It took all the will-power she possessed to leave the bedroom.

The apartment appeared to be deserted. Jemma made herself a cup of coffee in the stainless steel kitchen and wandered back into the living area, not sure what to do. Leave seemed a good option, she mused, just as Luke appeared, looking spectacular in a dark grey business suit, a paler grey shirt and silk tie. She had trouble tearing her gaze away, and had to battle down the blush that threatened.

'I was about to wake you, but you're dressed; good. My lawyer will be here in fifteen minutes so you can sign the pre-nup, and that's it.' Jemma was still digesting this comment when he walked across and smiled brilliantly down at her. 'Everything is ready for the wedding, honey.' He dropped a kiss on her brow. 'And if you haven't put your house up for sale yet, I can get my people to do it for you.'

He was so relaxed, so matter-of-fact. A night of passionate sex obviously had no more effect on him other than to put a satisfied smile on his face. Jemma realised she needed to learn quickly to do the same.

'No, that won't be necessary. I have it all in hand.' She didn't like to lie, but she was at a loss for anything else to say. She had made her bed and now she had to lie in it. After last night, lying in that particular bed wasn't going to be a hardship, but as for the rest of her life…

Luke's lawyer was super-efficient and insisted on reading out the whole of the pre-nuptial agreement to them. Basically, they both kept what they owned, but Jemma got nothing if they parted in the first three years of marriage—which wasn't surprising, considering Luke would be paying into Vanity Flair for the next three years. Afterwards, Luke left with the lawyer, telling her he would be back at six, leaving Jemma to finally go home.

*   *   *

Free of Luke's powerful presence for the first time in hours, Jemma glanced around the crowd of people in disbelief. They had been married in the gardens of Luke's house in Greece a few short hours before, and if this was what Luke called a simple party then she would hate to be around when he threw a big one.

Her father had given her away, with at least two hundred people present. Wearing a designer gown in ivory satin with a boned bodice, and nothing much else apart from a thong at Jan's insistence—because anything more would spoil the line of the slim-fitting skirt—Jemma had sat at Luke's side through a magnificent banquet set out on the vast terrace that ran the width of the house. After what had seemed like interminable speeches the music had started. Luke had led her out into the middle of the terrace and they had started the dancing.

Jemma let her glance rest for a moment on her new husband. Luke had been pulled into the middle of the floor by a group of men and they had all shed their jackets and ties and were dancing some traditional Greek dance together. The music and laughter were loud and their movements were very sexy, making her head spin. Hastily she looked away. Spotting a huge potted vine, she crossed to gently touch the leaves before walking around the plant to one of the huge marble columns that supported the upper balcony. She leant against it. She felt hot, and the shade plus the cool marble at her back were a welcome relief from the fierce heat.

She had done it…she was married…and everyone was happy. Theo certainly was. A brief smile spread across her tense features. Luke's grandfather's delight on seeing her when she had arrived yesterday, and his gentle charm, had done much to relieve her nervous tension at the thought of marrying Luke.

She had been given her own room last night, in deference to her wedding day and Theo's sensibilities as to what was correct—much to Luke's disgust. But Jemma had been glad of the breathing space, having spent the two nights before in Luke's bed. It was a lot harder than she had thought to match Luke's sophisticated attitude to sex.

Early this morning, much to her surprise, Theo had walked into her bedroom bearing a coffee tray. They had drunk coffee and he had told her that Luke was basically a good man and that he was sure his grandson loved her. But he'd also said he knew Luke could be overpowering in the pursuit of what he wanted, and that if Jemma had any doubts about marrying him she should say so now and Theo would understand.

She had reassured the old man, and apologised for lying to him in London when she had told him she had never seen Luke before, explaining away the lie by touching on Luke's attachment to Jan at the time. Theo had appeared to accept the story, but Jemma was convinced he saw a lot more than Luke gave him credit for.

'Excuse me?' Jemma glanced up and saw a strikingly attractive older man with a mane of white hair standing in front of her. 'I wonder if I may have a few words with you?'

'Yes of course. Mr Karadis, isn't it?' She remembered his name because when he had been in the receiving line earlier he had looked startled when he saw her. He had been accompanied by his wife and daughter, and a son about Luke's age in a wheelchair.

'You are—or were—Jemma Sutherland. No?'

'Yes, why?' His brown eyes darkened with some deep emotion, and Jemma wondered if it was wise to talk to a man she didn't know, but suddenly he smiled and his handsome face came alive.

'You are my beautiful Mary's…how do you say… niece, yes?'

Five minutes later there were tears in Jemma's eyes and she was clutching the man's hand with her own. He had been her aunt's lover for thirty years, and the son in the wheelchair was the reason why Mr Karadis had never left his wife. Jemma told him about her aunt's will, and the house on Zante, and his eyes filled with tears.

'Excuse a foolish old man, but meeting you and knowing you will keep her memory alive for me, and keep our secret, I am content.' And, leaning forward, he kissed her cheek. 'I can see her in your eyes, and if you ever, ever need anything at all, call on me.'

Where on earth was she? Luke walked towards the house and stopped. His bride of a few hours was lounging back against a marble pillar, holding hands with Karadis the banker and allowing him to kiss her cheek. A man she had only just met, and probably the only man in Greece who was as wealthy as Luke. What was it with Jemma and old men? Theo had taken one look at her and been smitten, and Karadis, renowned as a model of propriety, was obviously bowled over by her charm.

'So this is where you're hiding.' Jemma's head jerked up at the sound of Luke's voice, and saw his eyes narrow on the older man. He said something in Greek. Mr Karadis said something back, and then laughed before turning to Jemma.

'It has been a pleasure to meet you, Jemma, and now I must go. But I hope we meet again.'

Jemma smiled. 'So do I,' she said softly, and watched him walk away.

'Very touching. But do you have to hide away and flirt with every old man you meet?' Luke growled.

'I was not flirting, and nor was I hiding. I was trying to cool off.' Seeing Luke with sweat beading his forehead and his broad chest revealed by the open neck of his shirt did nothing to lower her temperature—quite the reverse. But if the past few days with Luke had taught her anything, it was a much better understanding of her aunt Mary. And now she and her aunt had a passion for handsome Greeks males in common, as well as their passion for plants, she thought, with a secretive smile curling her lips.

'If you say so.' He shrugged, but she could sense his underlying anger. 'You can cool off in the helicopter; it's time we said goodbye to our guests and left for Zante.' And, grasping her hand firmly, he led her back into the crowd of guests.

A short time later Jemma stepped out of the helicopter and glanced around. They had landed on a heli-pad on the roof of a building. 'Where are we?' she asked.

Luke took her arm and slanted her a sidelong glance. 'Our hotel.'

CHAPTER NINE

A TINGLING sensation the length of her spine woke Jemma from a deep sleep. It was a finger tracing her backbone, and slowly she opened her eyes to view of a broad, hair-roughened chest. Stretching, she sighed and rolled onto her back.

'At last you are awake.' Luke followed her over, his amused grey eyes gleaming down into hers. 'I was beginning to wonder if I would have to start without you.'

With the rock-hard length of him pressed against her thigh there was no mistaking his aroused state. 'You are insatiable,' Jemma murmured, smiling languorously up at him.

'Mmm, but morning arousal in the male is a fact of life—one we poor men have to deal with,' Luke said drolly, one hand reaching out to cup her breast.

'Is it really? I didn't know that.' Jemma sighed at the delicious sensations seeping through her.

'Then you must have been singularly unobservant of the men in your life. Which reminds me…' He paused, his hand now gently stoking over both her breasts in a figure eight. 'I had a word with Liz about your five a.m. starts, and we agreed it makes much more sense for the guy you employ to take the early-morning shifts.'

'You did what?' Jemma stiffened in outrage, no longer languorous but livid. 'You had no right to discuss my business behind my back. I'm perfectly happy with my hours as they are, and so was Liz until you put your oar in.'

Luke's hand stilled on her breasts. 'If I truly believed for a second that you and Liz were happy with the present arrangement I would not have interfered, but I know for a fact that Liz isn't mad about it. She only alternates the early start with you because of your friendship.'

Jemma stared at him in astonishment. 'She told you that? She's never said anything to me.'

'As I've told you before, Jemma, you have a great ability for burying your head in the sand and seeing only what you want to see.'

'But I asked her dozens of times if she minded,' Jemma muttered, all the fight draining out of her. 'And she always said no.'

'Probably because as a married woman with a baby she didn't want to take advantage of the situation and appear to be doing less than her share. But surely you realised that with a baby disrupting her sleep the last thing she needed was to get up at the crack of dawn to go to work?'

'Oh, hell!' Jemma swore. Why hadn't she insisted Liz forget the early starts? Because, if she were being brutally honest, Jemma wasn't really keen on them herself? 'You're right,' she said, feeling ashamed.

Luke's eyes lit with amusement, his hand resuming its caressing motion over her breasts. 'I usually am,' he teased. 'So, no more arguments.' His lips brushed lightly across her mouth, a fingertip scraping over a burgeoning nipple, and the teasing caresses eased her back into languorous pleasure again. 'But in consolation,' he husked, 'you were right about my being insatiable.' She saw the shadow of passion darken his chiselled features. 'And you love it, Jemma.' His mouth covered hers in a long, slow, sensuous kiss, and she had to acknowledge that she did...

Half an hour later she refused his offer to join him in the shower, her body still pulsing in the aftermath of his tender yet torrid lovemaking. For a moment she just lay there, staring into space and trying to analyse what had happened to her. It was now Monday morning and they hadn't left the suite since their arrival on Saturday night. In fact, they had hardly left the bed.

Luke had shown her a whole new dimension to her sexuality; one she had never known existed. She had loved Alan, and their first night together. She remembered crying afterwards, overcome with emotion at the wonder of his lovemaking. They had made love frequently, and if she hadn't reached orgasm very often it had never bothered her, so sure had she been of being loved. His death had almost torn her apart, the pain horrendous, and she never wanted to go through that again.

But Luke aroused no such emotion in her—certainly no desire to cry. In truth, as he had led her down the many erotic paths of sexuality with a skill and expertise that drove her mindless, her only emotion—if it could be called an emotion—had been a wild and reckless carnal need to devour him whole.

So what did that make her? Jemma wondered and, rising from the bed, she pulled on a towelling wrap and walked across to the window, to stare pensively out at the view of sand and sea. She heard the shower running and turned to stare at the bathroom door, her heartbeat increasing as she pictured Luke naked in the shower.

She answered her own question as she walked towards the bathroom. She was probably the perfect wife for a man like Luke, a notorious womaniser who saw marriage only as a business deal. They both wanted something from the union, but love did not come into the equation. Well, that suited Jemma just fine. And, opening the bathroom door, she shrugged off her robe and joined Luke in the shower stall.

*   *   *

Luke looked at the steps carved into the rock and then back at Jemma. 'Is this the only way down?'

'There's a jetty of sorts, and you can get to the house by boat, but otherwise this is it,' she said, grinning up at him. 'I hope you're fit.' She stepped past him to descend the steps.

'No—wait.' Luke grabbed her arm. 'Let me go first, then if you fall I can stop you.' He had no intention of losing his very new wife in a headlong fall onto the rocks below.

'My, what a gentleman,' Jemma teased, but did as he said.

Aunt Mary's house on Zante was a typical island cottage—all on one level, about twenty feet wide and forty feet long, and set in the middle of a narrow strip of land slightly higher than the beach. It had been extended a decade or so ago, quite simply, by adding another twenty feet to one end to create a comfortable living area, with floor-to-ceiling glass doors to take full advantage of the magnificent view.

'It's not as bad as I thought,' Luke remarked as they stopped outside the original door, and Jemma permitted herself a small smile. He was in for a shock... 'I've arranged for an architect to look over the place on Wednesday.' Which immediately knocked the smile off Jemma's face. She didn't want a stranger to see inside her aunt's house—and certainly not in Jemma's presence. She cringed with embarrassment at the very thought as she opened the door and led Luke through into the living area.

Jemma had seen it all before—the two huge soft cushioned cream sofas, a bit shabby after years of use, the glass-topped table supported by two dolphins, the small semi circular bar in one corner and the wall of book-filled shelves. But telltale signs of Aunt Mary were all around her, and the memories came flooding back. Restlessly she moved across to the window to stare sadly out to sea, and she wondered if her aunt would approve of what she had done.

Luke came up behind her and put his arm casually around her waist. She leant back against him, for once glad of his support. 'I don't see why you thought it wasn't fit to live in. It is a bit on the small side, but fine for holiday home. I can see now why Theo wanted to come back here. He was right about the cove, the view is spectacular.'

'Yes,' Jemma agreed, her gaze on the high cliffs that protruded about a hundred feet at either side of the small bay, protecting it from the worst of the elements. Her eyes rested on the opposite side, where a landing of sorts had been hewn out of the rock and a path led through the garden area back to the house.

'Come on—let's check out the bedrooms. Theo said there were two, but given the size of the building they will have to be extended and another couple added,' Luke suggested, turning her in his arms and looking deep into her eyes. 'I don't like to feel constrained in the bedroom,' he added wickedly.

A slight blush stained Jemma's cheeks. 'I know,' she murmured, her eyes darkening perceptibly, and he angled down his head and claimed her full, slightly parted lips, his tongue probing straight between them with the overwhelming eroticism of an expert.

The familiar sensual excitement lanced through her, and she closed her hands around the nape of his neck and pressed into the hard muscular wall of his chest, her breasts tingling with the contact. For a moment Jemma gave herself up to the physical pleasure only Luke could arouse in her. But only for a moment. A much better idea occurred to her and she slid her hands down between them and tore her mouth from his. She saw the puzzlement in his eyes and her lips curled in a mischievous smile.

'You wanted to see the bedroom,' she reminded him, and, twisting away, she chuckled as she darted through the big room to the hall.

Luke gave her a quizzical look as he stopped beside her. 'Why do I have the feeling you're up to something, Jemma?'

Still smiling, she opened the door to the bedroom and switched on the light, illuminating the shuttered room with a subdued glow. Theatrically flinging her arms wide, she said, 'Da-da...!'

'Oh, my God!' Luke exclaimed.

The expression on his face was priceless and Jemma laughed out loud. The original two bedrooms and bathroom had been knocked into one large room with an *en-suite* bathroom at the far end. The murals covering three walls depicted erotic naked figures from ancient Greek legend in incredible positions, and in intimate detail. The ceiling was draped in wild silk shot through with gold, and in the centre was a beaten gold canopy that was supported by snake-entwined gold poles, which was an intrinsic part of the huge circular bed beneath.

'Now I understand why you didn't want Theo to visit,' Luke said, drawing her against him, his appreciative gaze narrowing to shards of pure silver. 'But I don't understand why you thought it was unsuitable for you and I.'

Jemma's mouth ran dry, a wanton surge of heat igniting in her belly. 'Perhaps because I didn't know you so well when I said that,' she suggested huskily, and, slightly surprised at her own boldness, she wrapped her arms around him. The atmosphere between them sizzled with sexual tension.

'And now you do, shall we stay here a while?' Luke asked thickly.

'Oh, yes. I—' His tongue delved between her parted lips before she could finish the sentence. Clinging to him, she trembled in the circle of his arms as he lifted her up and, slipping off her sandals, placed her on the massive bed.

'Every time I look at you I want to strip you naked,' Luke confided. Whipping off his top and shorts, kicking off his beach shoes, he joined her on the bed. Then he laughed. 'A mirrored canopy; it gets better and better.'

'I know.' She ran her hand over his biceps and across, to linger sensually on the muscular swell of his chest as need surged inside her. She smiled as Luke reached for her.

'Much as I love your touch, now it is not a good idea. I want to take this slow.' And, taking her hand from his chest, he unbuttoned her blouse and slid it from her shoulders, his head dipping so his tongue could taste the tender crests of her breasts. She gasped.

'You are so receptive,' Luke told her huskily, taking the tie from her hair. Easing her flat on the bed, he took her shorts and panties from her body. The silver flame of his eyes wandered over her beautiful face, her slender shoulders, and, moving a long leg between hers, he leant back to stare down at her. The breath left Jemma's lungs when she registered the ferocious extent of his arousal.

'For you.' Luke smiled, a wickedly amused twist of his mobile mouth that was incredibly seductive. 'But not yet.' Reaching forward, he took her hands and spread them wide on each side of her body. 'Stay like that,' he commanded, as his gaze skimmed lower over her rose-tipped breasts to the red-gold curls at the junction of her thighs.

Jemma's hands curled into the soft silken sheets at her

sides but she did as he said, trembling like a leaf in the wind as his hands cupped her breasts and gently kneaded them. Then with finger and thumb he nipped the rigid tips until a whimpering moan of pure pleasure escaped her.

'Easy, Jemma. I want to take full advantage of this extraordinary room,' he said, and, leaning forward, he teasingly outlined the curve of her mouth with his tongue before slipping it inside with a wickedness that made her blood thicken and then flow like molten lava through her veins.

She lifted her arms to hold him, but he placed them back on the bed. 'No touching—not yet,' he decreed, before resuming toying with the rigid peaks of her breasts, this time with his mouth. The rhythmic suction sent ever strengthening sexual messages through her body until she cried out his name.

'You like that?'

'Yes,' she breathed as he leant back again, his hand moving lower to her stomach and the soft silken curls below, his fingertips slipping between the velvet folds and lingering there to tease and caress with subtle expertise. 'Oh, yes,' Jemma moaned, her writhing body on fire. Then, catching sight of the reflection in the mirrored roof of the canopy, she gasped.

She was splayed beneath him, a willing prisoner to the tormenting touch of his fingers. She saw the sheen of sweat on his sleek muscled body, the straining strength of his arousal. Shaking with the agonising ache of frustrated desire, she widened her eyes to molten gold pools of passion as Luke reared up and sank into the sleek, moist heat of her.

His powerful shoulders locked, and as he thrust hard and deep her control shattered. She clutched him, her fingers digging into his back, her internal muscles clenching around the entire length of him.

'Ah, Jemma,' he groaned, easing back.

'Don't stop,' she whimpered.

'No way.' He kissed her. 'But it's my turn to view.' He flipped her around to straddle him, silver fire burning away every trace of grey in his smouldering eyes as he reared up beneath her.

Jemma's head fell back as he rocked her to the very core, their bodies locked in a frantic primitive coupling. In a tangle of arms and legs he spun her around on the decadent bed with a thrusting driven passion that finally shattered his control. A rough groan was torn from his throat and the world exploded around Jemma in wave after wave of ecstasy so sublime she thought she might die of it. Dimly she was aware of sobbing out his name, then Luke was on top of her again, his great body rigid, racked with great shuddering convulsions as she was swept into a mindless oblivion.

When she opened her eyes Luke was lying across her with his head buried in the curve of her shoulder. She stared up and saw the reflection of his magnificent bronzed body, his skin beaded with sweat, his buttocks clenched, and felt the still throbbing length of him inside her. She closed her eyes again.

Some time later Luke's deep voice rasped against her ear. 'I'm too heavy—I don't want to flatten you into the bed.' And he rolled off onto his back.

Jemma slowly opened her eyes once more, and her eyes met his in the mirror above. 'You're not that heavy,' she murmured, letting her gaze wander down over his magnificent torso. 'But is that a suggestion of a paunch I spy?' she teased, glancing back at his face. She saw where his eyes were fixed and suddenly realised she was equally naked. She felt vaguely uncomfortable. It was one thing for lovers to be naked together, but there was something voyeuristic and slightly unpleasant about a mirrored bed.

'Cheeky.' Luke leant up on one elbow to look down at her. 'I'm a man in my prime.' He grinned. 'But your aunt must have been one heck of a woman, with a seriously erotic imagination.' His eyes caught sight of a particular picture on the wall and it almost made him blush—which would have been a first. 'Though I suppose it could have been her lover's idea.'

'You could be right about the fantasy thing. I know that it was after spending ten days sharing this room with my aunt last year that I fell into your bed on the yacht,' Jemma said dryly. 'Maybe it wasn't the wine. Maybe I received a subliminal message or something.'

Luke chuckled; he much preferred that scenario than wondering if she had used him as a substitute for her dead husband. Pure lust he could appreciate, as had the man who had paid for this love nest, he mused. 'Do you know who your aunt's lover was?' he asked idly.

'No, I have no idea.'

Luke's eyes narrowed on her supine body. Her fabulous hair was fanned out in a wild halo around her head, a few tendrils falling over her breasts, and a slight flush of pink was spreading over her skin and colouring her lovely face. Her glorious amber eyes avoided his and he knew she was lying. He could actually feel it in the slight tension of her body touching his own. But why? 'Your aunt never even gave you a hint?' he prompted, giving her a second chance to come clean.

'No.' Jemma sat up and swept her mass of hair back from her forehead. 'And it doesn't matter now she's dead.' She flicked him a glance. 'Do you realise we have ended up upside down on this bed?' she said, swinging her legs to the floor.

'There isn't a correct way round on a circular bed,' Luke pointed out with a slightly cynical smile, well aware that she had deliberately tried to change the subject and deciding to let it go. After all, it had nothing to do with him, but oddly it rankled that Jemma had lied; she obviously didn't trust him with the secret. But why should he care? She was married to him, and without conceit he knew the rampant desire that flared within him every time he looked at her was returned one hundred per cent by her. Their sexual compatibility was incredible. He only had to touch her and she was incapable of hiding her response—she didn't even try. But it didn't stop him wondering what other secrets she kept hidden from him...

'No, I suppose not.' Jemma forced a reciprocal grin to her lips and inexplicably she shivered. Suddenly the room seemed claustrophobic, and she had a terrific urge to get out. She found her shorts and panties and stepped into them, but she had to walk around the bed to find her shirt. When she did she slipped it on and fastened the buttons with fingers that shook.

Her smile was reassuring, until Luke saw the shadows in her eyes and the haste with which she dressed. Was she regretting their romp in the decadent bed? Or was she remembering her last husband and wishing it had been he she had shared the experience with? The unbidden thought popped into his head.

No—surely not. If Luke had learned anything about his beautiful wife in the last few days it was that for a woman who had been married before she was oddly inexperienced in the bedroom—though flatteringly eager to make love. He had felt it in her tentative touch, seen the shock in her eyes and felt the slight resistance as he had delved into the fiery curls between her legs with his tongue and tipped her into a shuddering climax. It was something she had never experienced before, she had confided breathlessly. He had heard it in her startled exclamation—*I didn't know that was possible*—after a particularly adventurous episode in the spa bath, and this morning in her assertion that she had never heard of male morning arousal. Perhaps her late husband hadn't had much of a sex drive.

He watched her slip her small pink-toed feet into her sandals. He loved her feet… His mind drifted away as his eyes slid up over her. He loved everything about her. Her glorious hair fell down her back in silken disarray, her face was free of make-up, glowing in the aftermath of sex, and the swollen contours of her lush lips made him want to kiss her again. Love her again…

Jemma had turned out to be an amazing lover.. shy, but growing bolder by the day. Remembering her laughter when she had thrown open the door of this room, the eagerness with which she had come into his arms, had him aroused again in an instant. His gaze dropped to her cleavage as she fumbled with the buttons of her shirt. He had never seen her wear a bra, but then she didn't need to. She was as natural as the flowers she adored, and, if anything, more exquisite than any specimen known to man. But she *had* known another man…

There it was again. The infantile curiosity to know what her last husband had been like as a lover. Damn it all, why was he bothered? It wasn't like him at all. With all the women he had known in his life he'd never had any desire to know about their previous partners, and he never discussed the women in *his* past. He knew he was a good lover, and he knew he made Jemma happy in bed; that was all that mattered, wasn't it…? He realised she had moved to the door. 'Leaving so soon?'

Jemma slanted him a glance over her shoulder. 'Yes. You've seen the place now, and we'll be back the day after tomorrow with the architect. You were right about the house; it will make a decent holiday home. But in my opinion it's not really suitable for Theo to live in; the access is far too difficult.' And without waiting for his response she opened the door and dashed down the hall out into the fresh air.

As she turned her back on him and shot out of the room it hit Luke like a blow to the solar plexus that keeping Jemma happy in bed was not all that mattered to him. He wanted more, much more. He wanted her to be incapable of walking away from him; he wanted to be the centre of her universe...

He, Luke Devetzi, who had never believed in love, was totally smitten. He had tried to deny it in his mind ever since their first encounter, because he had thought she was married. But suddenly he recognised the truth. He had been celibate for a year after meeting Jemma, and as a man who had never gone more than a couple of months without a woman since he was a teenager he should have realised something was wrong. It had been sheer desperation that had led him into dating Davina. But from the minute he'd seen Jemma again, and realised she was free, with single-minded determination he had plotted and planned and spent a fortune to make her his.

Stunned, he looked around the bedroom—a place designed by past lovers, exciting, but faded now, and certainly not essential to Luke. In fact, he didn't give a damn about the house—it was Theo's dream, not his—and yet he had used both it and her father's actions to force Jemma into marrying him.

Oh, hell... How could he hope she would fall in love

with him, given the way he had behaved? In fact, if this gut-wrenching terrified feeling was *love*, he wasn't sure he wanted it.

Jemma took a deep steadying breath as she walked slowly down to the water's edge.

'I take it an orgy is out, then?' Luke appeared at her side and she lifted her eyes to meet the dryly amused expression on his face.

'You've got that right,' she shot back smartly. 'I want to get back to our comfortable hotel and be waited on hand and foot.'

Luke took her face between his hands; her hair was loose and gleaming golden in the sun. Her eyes lifted slightly warily to his, for all her smart comment, and he wanted to tell her then how he felt, to see the wariness fade from her incredible eyes, see them glow with a deeper emotion. But he didn't. Instead he took her mouth with his own in a long tender kiss. Jemma was his now; he would do everything in his power to keep her, and that was all he needed to know...

CHAPTER TEN

BUT on Thursday, after Luke had shown Paul the architect around the house while Jemma had determinedly stayed outside, he wasn't so sure.

Paul was young, dark and handsome, and his eyes had lit up when he saw the bedroom. But they'd lit up a hell of a lot more when, after he had sketched a rough plan, they'd exited the house and found Jemma lying on a towel on the beach in a minuscule bikini.

It struck Luke that, much as he appreciated Jemma's fantastic body, he was nowhere near happy to see other men appreciate it as well. Nor was he at all pleased by the architect's rather sly aside in Greek, 'Are you sure you want to get rid of that bedroom?'

Luke gave him a gimlet eyed stare that knocked the smile from his face, and fixed his attention on his wife. 'You've had enough sun for one day, Jemma,' he snapped, and reached down a hand to pull her to her feet. Picking up the towel, he wrapped it around her shoulders. He saw the surprise and query in her amber eyes and realised he had sounded harsh. But then he had never suffered from jealousy before...

How are the mighty fallen, Luke thought, and smiled wryly down at her, wrapping her possessively in the curve of his arm. 'The architect has done a rough sketch; I'm sure you'll like it, Jemma.' And, indicating the garden and the jetty with his hand, he explained, 'The house will be extended on that side in an L shape, to provide four bedrooms, incorporating a boat house to end at the landing stage and solving the problem of Theo's safe arrival and departure.'

She glanced up at him through the thick veil of her lashes. 'You mean obliterate the garden and rockery?'

'Yes. It makes perfect sense. Don't you see?' he said with growing enthusiasm. 'That side catches the sun all afternoon, and a veranda will run along the length of the building for shade. The rest will be a paved courtyard, for dining out, and you can have potted palms, plants, flowering creepers, anything you like. There will be very little maintenance involved.'

'No,' she rejected bluntly, and, twisting out of his arm, she ignored Luke and said to Paul, 'Sorry, you'll have to think of some other way; perhaps a second storey on the house, or restoring the original two bedrooms?'

Luke was puzzled and a little put out at her instant dismissal of the plan. 'Be sensible, Jemma, that's the only spare land there is. And as I recall you damaged your fingers building the rockery. The garden isn't necessary with the natural beauty of the bay all around.'

'It is to me,' she said flatly, avoiding his gaze.

He knew she loved gardening, but she was being ridiculous and he was becoming annoyed. 'It's all right,' he said to Paul. 'Show my wife the sketch and I'm sure when she realises how stunning it will be she'll agree.' But, to his amazement, Jemma took the sketch that Paul held out to her, glanced at it, and then tore it into little pieces.

'I'm afraid my husband has misled you, Paul. This house is mine, and only mine, and if there are any alterations to be done they will be ordered and approved by me, and only me. Isn't that right, Luke?' she demanded, lifting hard angry eyes to his. 'As I recall, it's set out as such in our pre-nup,' she reminded him scathingly. 'You keep what's yours and I keep what's mine. And now, if you will excuse me, I'm going for a swim.' Shrugging off the towel, she ran down the beach and into the sea.

Luke felt like strangling her, he was so furious, but instead he had to escort the architect off the property, promising he would be in touch later. By the time he had walked to the top of the cliff and then made the descent back to the beach Luke had had plenty of time to think, and his temper had cooled somewhat.

He was an astute man, he had made a fortune reading the stock market, and he brought the same sharp intelligence to bear now in reading Jemma. She was sexy as hell, but she was also a sweet, lovable, loyal woman. It was obvious in the way she behaved with everyone she met. The staff in the hotel adored her—he had caught her this morning asking the porter how his new baby was. She had the capacity to be at ease with anyone, and, although Luke had given her no choice but to marry him, she had accepted it and without too many arguments more than fulfilled her part of the deal.

He had never had such mind-blowing sex with a woman in his life, and still he couldn't get enough of her. In fact, the force of his feelings frightened him; it wasn't just the physical connection with Jemma, but almost a mental connection. He loved her, and he had never felt anything like it in his life.

Which was why he knew it was not in Jemma's nature to react so furiously over something so simple as a sketch suggesting an extension to the house. His grey eyes narrowed and he glanced around the cove, his gaze lingering on the garden. So what was so important about the garden that it upset her so badly?

Stripping off his clothes to reveal black Speedo trunks, he walked towards the water. Like Aphrodite rising from the waves she stood up, flicking the long length of her hair over one shoulder as she bent her head and wrung out the excess water, then straightened up. He saw her tense the moment she spotted him, and then reluctantly begin to walk towards him.

They met at the water's edge. His grey eyes darkened momentarily. God, she was gorgeous! But he shook his head; sex wasn't the answer this time. He wanted to know what had made her behave so out of character just now.

'Paul has left, and he won't be back until you say so.' He reached for her hand and linked his fingers through hers. 'You and I need to have a talk.'

'That sounds ominous.' She tried to laugh, but he put a silencing finger over her mouth. He led her to where the towel was spread on the sand and, sitting down, pulled her down beside him, clamping her to his side with an arm around her waist. 'Really, Luke, I need to dress— you said yourself I've had too much sun.'

'You're not going anywhere until you tell me why you were so adamant that the garden couldn't be built on.' She looked up into his eyes, hers frankly wary. 'I know this house was given to your aunt by the man she was having an affair with, but what I don't understand is why you care what happens to the place. By your own admission this is only the second time you have visited the house, so it has to be your aunt's secret you're protecting.'

Jemma shuddered; Luke was practically naked, and though she had lost a lot of her inhibitions in the last week—inhibitions she hadn't even known she had until Luke became her lover—she was having enough trouble breathing, never mind trying to think up a plausible lie for her earlier behaviour.

Steel-grey eyes sought hers. 'Don't even bother to try,' Luke said, his lips quirking at the corners in a smile.

'Your eyes give you away every time. Try trusting me instead.'

Trusting Luke… That was a novel concept, and not one she had ever considered.

'I promise your secret will be safe with me,' he added.

Oddly, she believed him. Although he was an extremely powerful tycoon, renowned for the ruthlessness that had made him a multimillionaire before he was thirty, and with enough sexual charisma to seduce any woman on the planet, Jemma sensed an incorruptible air of inner strength about him.

Something he had inherited from his grandfather maybe? she thought. Or perhaps that was just wishful thinking on her part. Because with his arm protectively around her waist and his faint male scent surrounding her senses she had an incredible urge to confide in him. For over a year she had been the sole guardian of her aunt's secret, and it weighed heavily on her.

Luke looked down at her, his eyes gleaming silver-grey beneath his thick lashes. 'You have an English saying, no? A trouble shared is a trouble halved?' He read her mind. 'And I am a very good listener,' he said persuasively.

'You're never going to let this rest, are you?' She sighed, and, clasping her hands together, she told him.

'Twenty years ago my aunt was expecting a baby by her lover. She was five months pregnant when they sailed into Zante for a lovers' tryst, as they had done countless times before, but she slipped and fell when stepping off the boat. She miscarried the baby within the hour. It happened too quickly to get help—not that it would have done any good. The baby was a girl, and she and her lover buried the poor mite at the base of the cliff and put a few stones there to mark the spot. Aunt Mary told me that there was nothing illegal about what they did. If it had happened in a hospital in those days the child would have simply been discarded. But to my aunt her baby was real, a symbol of her lifelong commitment to her lover. She really wanted a gravestone, but that wasn't an option, so instead I built the rockery as a memorial, and I also promised to preserve the baby's resting place.' Jemma's eyes filled with moisture as she remembered her aunt's pain-racked face as she had told her the story.

Luke was not a sentimental man, but even he could understand why the house had been left in trust the way it had—the woman hadn't been able to leave it to her own child, so she'd left it to Jemma's children, and to her children's children… Whether it was fair to Jemma, he wasn't so sure. He saw the sadness in her expressive face and slid the fingers of his free hand gently through the tangled mass of her hair and turned her to face him. Then he saw the tears in her eyes, and he drew in a deep breath. 'Don't say any more, sweetheart, I understand.' Brushing his lips across her brow, he tightened his arm around her waist and hugged her close, stroking his other hand up and down her back in an age-old gesture of comfort.

Held in the warmth of Luke's arms, relief at having shared the burden was Jemma's primary emotion. 'Do you really understand, I wonder?' she murmured softly. 'You don't believe in love, and maybe that's the best way to be; it only causes pain.' She barely noticed Luke's hand fall from her back, and she didn't see the sudden tightening of his lips.

'My aunt spent her whole life loving a man she could never have and wanting a family that was never to be. Instead she had to make do with a few weeks a year with her lover. How tragic is that?' Jemma glanced around the bay. 'This place is an absolute Eden, but perhaps there's a serpent here somewhere.'

'Now you're just being fanciful,' Luke reprimanded with a wry smile. 'Your aunt chose her lifestyle, and it wouldn't have mattered where she was.'

His smile was beguiling, as was the warmth of his body. But Jemma knew Luke's view on *choice* all too well; it was the reason she was sitting here, married to him. And here she was telling him all her innermost secrets!

'Believe what you like,' she said, panicking at her own weakness in confiding in him. Twisting out of his hold, she rose to her feet. 'But I just have this feeling that the house is unlucky. I mean, it wasn't lucky for Aunt Mary, and it didn't bring much luck to Theo either, did it? He had to leave it when your mother got pregnant, and then she died very young. Now there's only you and Theo left—not much of a family, really.'

Luke got to his feet and stared at her for long tense seconds, the line of his jaw taut. Some emotion she didn't recognise darkened his eyes, and then he made a visible effort to relax and smile. 'Forget about the house for now. You and I are going to get off this island and spend the rest of our holiday cruising on my yacht and working on expanding my woefully small family.'

The sound of the shower running woke Jemma from a deep sleep. She stretched and yawned and pulled the fine cotton sheet up over her breasts. She glanced at the clock on the bedside table and groaned; it was barely six a.m. Then she remembered it was Monday—Luke was taking an early-morning flight to New York. Given the time difference, it meant he would be in New York in time for a business lunch. He'd been going to leave last night, but had changed his mind, and her body's well-used muscles reminded her why.

The door of the *en-suite* bathroom opened and Jemma's gaze automatically turned to her husband of four months. He was naked except for a towel slung low around his lean hips. His thick black hair was still damp from the shower, and a stray droplet of water was easing its way down his strong throat. He was six feet plus of pure masculine perfection, thought Jemma, taking a sudden, much-needed breath of air as she belatedly realised she'd stopped breathing when he'd entered the room.

'I know that look, Jemma.' Grey eyes met hers. 'But I have to be in New York by noon and you've delayed me once already.' With that remark, he disappeared into the dressing room.

Jemma stirred restlessly on the bed, punching the pillows and sitting up to rest against them. She should be happy that Luke was leaving—one of the reasons she had married him was because he'd agreed to her demand to stay in England, and she had counted on him not being around much. Except that it hadn't worked out quite as she'd expected.

On returning to London after their honeymoon, Jemma had found a new Volvo estate car waiting for her—a wedding present from Luke. He said he'd already noticed her car was well past its sell-by date. In the ten days he had spent in London before flying to the Far East he had managed to make friends with Liz and Peter. He had offered Peter a job in his company, and he hadn't stopped there. With Liz's enthusiastic support, he had advised them that Flower Power should take on at least two new assistants to cover the new contract they had won, and also that, as the owners, they should adopt a more hands-off position and work much fewer hours. Jemma's attempts to object had been futile; Luke was like a juggernaut, driving everyone his way.

Her only success had been the house on Zante. It was being altered as she had suggested—but only because when Luke had returned from the Far East a week later he had whisked her back to Greece for a few days, insisting they both had to take Theo to Zante and get his agreement to her proposal. She had been relieved to see that the erotic bedroom had been stripped before they'd arrived. The house was now going to have a first floor, with four *en-suite* bedrooms, and was to be used as a holiday home.

'Home' was an emotive word, she mused, glancing around the bedroom now. Did she consider this apartment home? She didn't know. All she did know was that Luke didn't travel half as much as she had been led to believe.

As man and wife their sex was great, but on a personal level they were no closer now than they had been on their wedding day—and that was fine by her. No, that wasn't quite true. They had developed a friendship of sorts, she supposed.

Their Christmas holiday in Greece with Theo had been fun, and they had been back in London now for three days. On Saturday night Luke had presented her with a diamond bracelet and insisted that they celebrate their four-month anniversary with dinner and, surprisingly, a trip to the opera—which she liked, but knew he didn't—and sex, of course.

He was always buying her presents. She had more jewellery than she knew what to do with, and the same was true of clothes. He was incredibly generous, and would not take no for an answer, and she was finally beginning to realise how fabulously wealthy he was.

Personally, she didn't care about money as long as she

had enough to live on, but she had a suspicion there would soon be someone else to consider. She hadn't told Luke yet, but her period was three weeks overdue.

Her original rosy plan of having his baby to bring up as she liked, because he would not be around that much to interfere, now seemed rather foolish. A slight frown marred her smooth brow. Luke had infiltrated into every aspect of her life, and she knew he would do the same with any child they had.

'Frowning? I'm flattered.' Jemma's head turned as Luke walked towards her. 'Dare I hope that you're going to miss me?' he drawled, silver eyes flaring for an instant as his glance swept her from head to toe. Belatedly she realised the sheet was around her thighs.

She drew in a startled breath, grasping the sheet and pulling it over her breasts, more flustered than his glance warranted. Luke had cured her of all her inhibitions in the bedroom, but she was off balance because the first thought that had popped into her head in answer to his question was yes, she would miss him.

He stopped by the bed, but she didn't trust herself to speak. Inwardly confused, she kept her gaze fixed on his body, rather than his face, but it wasn't much help. His exquisitely tailored navy jacket hung perfectly from his wide shoulders, a crisp cotton shirt covered his muscular chest and his long, elegant fingers, which had caressed every inch of her, were slipping a silk tie under the shirt collar. Dear heaven, she couldn't possibly miss him. She couldn't be falling in love with him. She wouldn't let it happen.

'You could come to New York with me—a phone call is all it would take, and I can delay leaving for the airport for half an hour to give you time to get ready,' he offered casually.

Jemma looked up in surprise. Luke always flew first class, and she had no doubt any airline would bump someone off a plane if they had to rather than say no to Luke Devetzi. But the fact that he had asked her to go with him threw her into a panic. 'No, I couldn't possibly; I have to go to work.'

'With the new staff your presence in the shop is hardly needed,' he pointed out. 'Humour me this time, hmm? I rather like the idea of showing you around New York.'

That he was asking her to humour him, travel with him, astonished her. The trouble was that for a moment she was seriously tempted, and it terrified her. 'No, travelling with you isn't part of our deal.'

'Of course it isn't.' Something bleak moved in the depths of his eyes, and then it was gone. 'How foolish of me to forget.' He leant down and pressed a brief, hard kiss on her lips. 'I'll be back in two weeks; try not to miss me too much...' he said mockingly, and, spinning on his heel, he left.

Jemma sat in the workshop feeling like hell. After Luke had left she'd been eating her breakfast when the phone rang. It had been Theo, for Luke, and when she told him he'd already left Theo had said, 'I only wanted to wish him a happy thirty-eighth birthday.' Jemma's laugh had been hollow. She'd told him she'd have to cut the conversation short because she was due at work.

'What's the matter with you?' Liz walked up to the bench and eyed Jemma with a worried frown. 'Are you missing Luke?'

'Something like that.' Jemma glanced up at her friend and decided to confide in her. 'Today is his birthday, and I forgot to wish him happy birthday before he left this morning.'

'Not good,' Liz said dryly. 'But not a complete disaster. Ring him up tonight and apologise, and then have telephone sex. That should do the trick—the man adores you.'

Jemma couldn't help smiling. 'I never realised you had such a salacious mind.'

'I didn't think you would appreciate it until you married a hunk like Luke.' Liz laughed, and Jemma frowned, the throwaway comment disturbing her a little.

Had her marriage to Alan not qualified her for the sexy wives' club? Suddenly she realised she had hardly thought about Alan in ages, and when she had, it had been with a sadness that he had died so young. The fond memories that she had of their marriage made her smile gently when she remembered them, rather than cry.

She thought of Luke and his request that she should accompany him to New York, and her refusal. She saw him in her mind's eye, standing by the bed, totally self-assured, his usual arrogant self. She felt again the brief, hard kiss and saw his mocking smile, the tension in his shoulders when he abruptly turned his back on her and left, and suddenly Jemma felt terribly guilty. What kind of wife was she not to have known it was his birthday—and he far too proud to tell her?

Luke rose from his desk, snapped his briefcase shut and glanced morosely around his office. For the amount of work he had done today he might as well have stayed at home. But where exactly was home? Anywhere his sexy wife was... He had grown to actively dislike the London apartment because it had slowly dawned on him that, although Jemma was there, she hadn't made the slightest effort to imprint her own personality on the place. Not a picture, not a flower had she added. The apartment was as stark as Theo had once suggested—nothing at all like the cosy house Jemma had shared with her first husband.

Luke sighed. As birthdays went, his had been a bummer. From the moment he had asked Jemma to come with him this morning—only for her to turn him down flat and remind him that travelling with him wasn't part of their deal—he had been in a black mood. He had hoped Jemma had got over the circumstances of their marriage, but obviously she hadn't.

Crossing to the bar, he poured himself a shot of Scotch into a crystal glass and with it in his hand he walked across to the window to stare moodily out over the New York skyline. He couldn't blame Jemma for the way she felt. He had made a deal to marry her, and she had stuck to it. If anyone had told him six months ago that he would marry and then fall in love with his wife, to the point where he neglected his work, he would have laughed in their face.

But the joke was on him. He had done everything in his power to get Jemma to care for him. He had sent her flowers from Japan the first time they were apart, and had been told on his return not to bother again because she owned a florist's shop. He had bought her jewellery, clothes—anything she wanted she could have. The trouble was she didn't want anything from him. Except sex.

Most men would be happy with an ever-willing wife, and yet even in that area he was getting increasingly desperate. In the physical sense she gave him everything, but slowly it had dawned on him that there was an intrinsic part of herself that she was keeping hidden from him.

Loving her had weakened him. He had neglected his business to a large extent already. Ordinarily he would not have spent more than a couple of weeks in London over the last four months, and instead he had spent most of his time there—with Jemma…

The sex was addictive, and he didn't want to give it up, wasn't even sure he could… But now he knew that love was even more addictive, and it was time he made a decision. To carry on as he was, but reorganise his workload to centre on London. Maybe buy a bigger house there and be content with what he had—or cut and run. Straightening his shoulders, he saw his face reflected in the window and grimaced. God, he was becoming maudlin—and why? Because his wife had forgotten his birthday.

No, Jemma hadn't forgotten, he amended. She didn't know when his birthday was because she had never cared enough to ask. But he could have told her this morning—except that his pride hadn't let him. How infantile was that?

A knock on the door broke into his mood of introspection. Who the hell was that? Everyone had left for the evening…

'Surprise, surprise!' Davina Lovejoy appeared in the doorway, waving a bottle of champagne. 'Happy birthday, darling.'

'Thank you,' he replied. She looked as beautiful as usual, but knowing the artifice involved in achieving that look was more than a bit off-putting. But at least she knew it was his birthday.

'Open this.' She placed the hand with the bottle in it against his shirtfront and smiled up at him. 'We can have a celebratory drink as old friends, and then I can wish you a happy birthday properly.'

There was nothing remotely proper about the invitation in the smiling eyes she lifted to his. He ignored the invitation, but was too much of a gentleman to refuse the drink. Taking the bottle, he popped the cork and crossed to the bar to find two glasses.

The phone on his desk rang. 'Shall I get that?' Davina asked, and without bothering to wait for a response lifted the receiver. 'Luke Devetzi's office, Davina here. Can I help you? Who did you say you were? Luke's wife—?'

'Jemma!' Luke tore the receiver from Davina's hand. She'd never called him before—something must have happened. 'What's wrong?'

'Nothing—nothing at all,' came the reply, and he felt a complete sense of euphoria when she added, 'Sorry to disturb you, Luke. I'm only ringing to wish you a happy birthday. I didn't know it was your birthday until Theo rang this morning to speak to you, and I feel awful I didn't get you a present. But I'll get you one before you come back. I thought perhaps a new briefcase or something. Or whatever you want. You can decide.'

Luke had never known Jemma to babble on like this, and she hadn't finished yet. But just to hear her voice was a pleasure, and his earlier worries faded like snow on a fire.

'Or maybe I should just surprise you; would you prefer that? Look, I'll ring off now; you're obviously busy at the moment,' she finished with a rush.

'No, I'm not. My PA just surprised me with a celebratory glass of champagne.' He glanced at Davina and gestured with his hand for her to leave. 'But she's leaving now.' Luke settled himself in the chair behind his desk, mouthing the word 'out' at Davina, who shrugged and left, slamming the door behind her. 'She's gone now, and I'm finished for the day. I was just about to leave.'

'Oh, well, I'll not keep you.'

'Yes, you will. Don't you dare put the phone down,' he ordered. 'I'm delighted you called to ask me what I want for my birthday. You naked in bed would be a good start.' He heard her gasp and let his imagination run riot as he told her exactly what he wanted and where.

Jemma had worried over ringing Luke all evening, and it had been almost midnight when she had picked up the phone and dialled his number. But allowing for the time difference she knew it was still early evening there. Overcome with nerves, she knew she had been babbling like a lunatic. But now, listening to Luke murmuring sexy suggestions in her ear, she was shocked.

'Luke—please,' she said breathlessly. 'You shouldn't say things like that on the telephone!' But it didn't stop her temperature rising and heat pooling in her belly. 'It's late, and I'm going to bed now.'

'To think of me, I trust,' he prompted, and she heard the smile in his voice.

'Yes, I think you can safely say that's a foregone conclusion after your very descriptive flights of fantasy,' she quipped, and heard him laugh.

'Good, because I'm destined to spend all evening in a cold shower! I'll try and get back sooner than two weeks, even if it's only for a day. In the meantime, perhaps you could check out the housing market. I've thought of something else I want. I know you don't really like the apartment, so I want you to look around for a house out of town with a large garden; that would suit you much better.'

For a moment Jemma was silent as the full import of his suggestion sank in. He wanted them to move to the country and settle down, and the idea thrilled her. She heard him say her name, ask if she was still there. She placed a hand on her stomach and said, 'Yes, Luke, I'll do as you say. Goodnight.' And she put the phone down.

Across the Atlantic Luke grinned and poured himself a glass of champagne. With the sound of Jemma's voice lingering in his head, his birthday had improved one hundred per cent.

CHAPTER ELEVEN

ON THURSDAY afternoon, Emma turned the key in the lock, opened the door, and walked into her old home in Bayswater carrying a cardboard box. It had the empty feel and the cold smell of a house no longer lived in. Not surprisingly, as she had only visited a couple of times before Christmas while Luke was abroad.

She shrugged off her coat and then wandered around the silent rooms for the last time. She had made the decision on Tuesday morning, after a sleepless night tossing and turning in the huge bed thinking of Luke. Jemma had taken a long hard look at herself, and she hadn't liked what she'd seen. She'd accepted the hope of a baby and great sex as a basis for marriage and consciously avoided any deeper commitment. She'd been so determined not to get involved with Luke on anything other than a superficial level that she hadn't even known it was his birthday. It wouldn't have hurt her to have asked him when it was, she realised guiltily.

When had she become so afraid of emotional involvement? With hindsight, she could see it had started after her mother had died. She hadn't made much attempt to get close to her stepmother and stepsister, preferring to cling to Aunt Mary and Alan. When she had lost Alan she'd been devastated, and losing her aunt the following year had simply compounded her problem. She was naturally a compassionate, caring person, but she had avoided developing deeper relationships with people and never dated men. She'd pushed away anyone who might pierce the wall she'd deliberately built around her deeper emotions. Anyone like Luke! She had been too frightened to allow him to get close, too scared of the pain that might follow if she lost him as well.

As dawn was breaking Jemma had finally realised that she had to let go of the past, let go of her fear, and not allow it to blight what could be a great future with Luke. She might very well be pregnant, and her child deserved a whole woman for a mother, not an emotional cripple.

Yesterday she had sadly discovered she wasn't pregnant, but it didn't change her mind. She had to move on, with hope for the future. She had already consulted an estate agent to enquire about a house in the country, as Luke had suggested, and to finally put her own house on the market. The valuer was coming around tomorrow, and she had nipped out from her stint at the shop this afternoon to collect the personal items she held dear—family photos, pictures from her childhood with her parents, her aunt and Alan—a photographic tapestry of her life so far. Hopefully one day she would have a baby and be able to show her child the family it belonged to.

She placed the box on the table in the living room and began packing, something she ruefully admitted she should have done months ago. She lingered over one or two items, and laughed and sighed over a few more. She glanced around the room and realised there was nothing else she wanted except a few mementos she kept in a drawer in the bedroom. Then a quick dust and a run over with the vacuum cleaner and she would be finished.

Jemma didn't hear the front door open, or the sound of someone mounting the stairs. She was sitting on the bed poring over a battered tin box holding her childish mementos of the past. An assortment of shells she had collected on summer holidays spent with her parents. A heart-shaped stone with a red ionised vein running through it in the same heart shape—a quirk of nature and as beautiful as any jewel made by man. Her eyes misted with tears as she recalled the day she had found it. Her father had been too busy at work, so Jemma and her mother had gone to Brighton for the day together and Jemma had dug the stone out of the sand. It was the last outing she had had with her mother before she died.

Wiping the tears from her eyes with the back of her hand, she sighed, closed the box and got to her feet. There was no sadness any more, only beautiful memories. She turned towards the door—and stopped.

Luke was framed in the doorway, dressed casually in a dark blue cashmere sweater and navy trousers, and her heart jumped in surprise and pleasure. 'What are you doing here? I wasn't expecting you back for another ten days?' she said with a smile.

The grey eyes were enigmatic as they surveyed her, but there was something in the slow twist of his mouth that made her inexplicably nervous. 'I thought I'd surprise you, and when you weren't at the apartment I called Flower Power. Patty told me you'd gone to your house in Bayswater,' he said smoothly. 'I thought you'd sold it long ago—but then I should have known you never had any intention of giving up this shrine to your last husband.'

'No, you're wrong.' She hastened to correct him.

'Am I?' Luke asked, walking towards her, his grey eyes sliding insolently over her. Something dark leapt to life in their depths as he viewed the rumpled but made up bed. 'You probably sleep here every time I'm away.'

'I don't,' Jemma quickly denied. His face was rigidly controlled, but she sensed anger simmering beneath the surface, and was perplexed by it. 'I only came today to collect a few mementos because the estate agent is due tomorrow.'

A black brow arched sardonically. 'Odd, but I seem to recall you telling me you saw an estate agent last year.'

Jemma flushed guiltily. 'Yes, well, that was a mistake. I never quite got around to it.'

'Don't bother lying, Jemma. I've heard it all before,' he jeered, and his hand snaked out, catching her wrist in an iron grip and pulling her towards him.

'It wasn't really a lie. But at the time you were rushing me,' she tried to explain, aware of feeling pleasure as his hard muscled thigh pressed against hers.

'I rushed you? I seem to remember you fell into my bed the minute you set eyes on me, and you didn't take much persuading the next time, either,' he said in a bitter tone of voice. For the first time she saw exactly how furious he was, and a frisson of apprehension ran down her spine. 'What do you take me for? A gullible fool? I come second best to no man—living or dead.'

Jemma stared back at him. Such anger over a tiny fib... Could it be that he was jealous? 'I never—'

'Shut up!' he snarled. 'I can't stand to hear any more of your lies. You hang on to your past love like a limpet. But your body has no such hang-ups, does it, my sweet wife?' He hauled her hard against him, the strong planes of his face taut with some dark emotion. 'I could have you on that bed in a heartbeat.'

Luke's long fingers came up to hold her head so that she couldn't move an inch.

'Luke, please...' she gasped in a low shaky tone.

Before she could say another word his mouth slammed down on hers, opening her lips and feasting on the sweetness within. When at last he released her mouth she tried to jerk away, trembling from head to foot, but, taking her by surprise, he tipped her back onto the bed.

The breath was knocked out of her body, and anger surged up inside her. Whatever she had done to enrage him, and whether he was jealous or not, she didn't care. She was damned if she was going to let him manhandle her. She struggled to sit up, but he came down on top of her, pinning her beneath him.

'Luke!' she cried.

'Yes, say my name.' His smile was chilling. 'I want you to know who it is that's taking you in this bed of cherished memories. You won't ever be able to sleep in it again without thinking of me.'

She put her hands between them, trying to push him away, but hardly moved the solid wall of his chest. His mouth descended on hers again, probing her lips apart and plundering them with a voracious passion. She could taste the anger in him, hear it in the thudding beat of his heart, feel it in the tension in his huge frame. Her eyes closed as his hands tore at her clothes. Her shirt was ripped open, her trousers unfastened and his hands feverishly caressed her flesh. His mouth was working havoc on her throat, her shoulders, her breasts, and she moaned out pleas for him to stop even as the familiar wild excitement flowed through her veins.

A muscled thigh thrust between her legs and he moved between them, his mouth ravishing hers yet again with a driven urgency that she wantonly met and matched. She was thrown into a vortex of passion, her head thrashing from side to side as her mouth opened on a groan of pure pleasure. Her hands reached frantically for him, one tangling in the thick black hair of his head, the other sliding beneath his sweater to feel the rapid thud of his heart, the warmth of his flesh. She was aware of the hard length of him moving purposely against her, the heat of their bodies at explosive pitch, when suddenly he stopped.

For a moment he lay still on top of her, dragging in ragged breaths, and slowly she raised her lids to look at him. He was watching her, his colour dark and his eyes fierce. 'What the hell am I *doing*?'

Drunk on passion, her body achingly aroused, she widened her eyes in shocked disbelief as he stood up and straightened his sweater over his trousers.

He stared grimly down at her and shoved his hands in his pockets. 'And to think I thought I might lo—' He stopped and shook his head. 'Thank God I found out in time. You're no better than any woman who's sold herself to the highest bidder.'

'That's a despicable thing to say!' Jemma cried, jerking up into a sitting position, but he avoided her gaze. Hopelessly confused, she asked, 'What's wrong with you?' and hated the plaintive tone in her voice.

'Can't you guess? I found you *here*, in your late husband's bed, *crying*.'

'I wasn't crying—' she began, but he wasn't listening.

'There's a Proverb—"Hope deferred maketh the heart sick". And I'm sick of you,' he ground out. Something shrivelled inside Jemma. 'I want a separation. You can stay here—it's obviously where you belong.' He gave her a sardonic glance. 'I was mad to think otherwise. I'll have your things sent over from the apartment. You can keep your allowance and do what you like with it. I don't want to see you ever again.'

She looked at him and saw disgust in his glacial eyes, in the hard, cold line of his mouth—the mouth that had driven her wild a moment ago—and ice seeped into her veins. She turned away from him and, fastening her trousers, slid her legs over the side of the bed. She had wanted

Luke just now with a hunger and need that shamed her, and finally she admitted to herself what she had known from the day she'd met him.

Alan had never made her feel this way. Their love had been born of a long friendship, gentle and caring. But Luke dominated her thoughts and her body to the exclusion of all else. She had spent all her energy in maintaining a barrier between them and now, when it was too late, it struck her like a knife through the heart—she loved Luke.

The pain started then, but Jemma refused to let him see how much he had hurt her. She pulled the remnants of her shirt up over her shoulders, fastened the one remaining button, and rose to her feet. It took every bit of will-power she possessed to lift her eyes to his. 'As you like,' she said, and she even managed to pull off a shrug. 'So long as our separation doesn't affect my father or the company.'

'Your father and the company will continue to have my monetary support, as agreed.' His mouth twisted. 'And if there's any chance you're pregnant, we'll have to come to some amicable arrangement.'

'No, I'm not pregnant. And tell Theo not to worry—he can stay at the house on Zante any time he likes.' So the irony was that the only person who'd not got what they wanted out of this marriage was her.

'Thank you, but I insist on paying you rent when he's there. Theo doesn't need to know.'

She stared at him, angry that he could even suggest paying her, but before she could reply Luke had spun on his heel and was gone.

Jemma sat back down on the bed, her eyes dry, trying to make sense of what had just happened. Luke had left for New York with no hint that anything was wrong, and that evening when she had called him…

She drew in a ragged breath. A woman had answered his phone. Davina— The name niggled at the back of her mind and then she remembered. According to Jan, the girl Luke had been dating before he'd married Jemma was called Davina somebody or other, and lived in New York. Suddenly Jemma saw it all. Luke must be back with Davina, and everything Luke had said over the phone when she'd called him on his birthday had been a sick joke—the sexy words Luke had murmured probably meant for the woman standing next to him in his office that evening. Had the two of them been laughing at her behind her back? When Luke had told Jemma to look for a country house with a garden because he knew the apartment did not suit her, she had naïvely thought he'd meant for them to share the new house. But instead it had been a hint for Jemma to move out of the apartment, to leave it free for him to move his other woman in.

What a blind fool she had been. Luke had another woman. If she were honest, it was no more than she had expected from the beginning. She supposed she should consider herself lucky their marriage had lasted four months. But she didn't consider herself lucky at all. And she blinked and blinked again but could not hold back the tears…

Luke climbed into his car and slammed the door shut, his chest heaving. He started the engine and then gripped the steering wheel with hands that shook. He had to get away, as far and as fast as he could. He was appalled at his own behaviour; he had damn near taken Jemma without thought or consideration for what she wanted. He had never felt such all-consuming anger in his life. She obsessed him to the point of insanity.

He had given Jemma everything, and ached for her love, and last night it had come to him after three frustrating days in the U.S.—the one thing he had not done was tell her he loved her. He had immediately chartered a plane and arrived in London determined to do so, with some romantic picture in his mind that she would fling herself into his arms and reciprocate his feelings.

As soon as Patty had told him Jemma was in Bayswater he had known, but he hadn't wanted to believe it. When he'd walked into the bedroom and seen her crying over her dead husband he had lost it completely. Love had made a raging idiot of him—but no more. In every other area of his life he was a resounding success, but with Jemma he had failed. He no longer trusted himself anywhere near her. She was a weakness he could no longer afford, and he'd had no option but to finish it—before his passion for her destroyed him.

A week later, Jemma was sitting in a restaurant with Liz, pretending to enjoy a lunch she had no stomach for.

'Cheer up, Jemma. Luke will be back on Saturday.' Liz grinned. 'Think of the pleasure in store.'

Jemma tried to smile and failed. What was the point? The truth had to come out some time? 'No, he won't, Liz. It's over.'

'No—I don't believe it; Luke worships you!'

'You know his reputation; he worships women in the plural,' Jemma said dryly. 'But never only one for very long, and I'm certain he has someone else.'

'Luke wouldn't do that to you; you must be mistaken,' Liz protested.

'I'm not mistaken. I saw him last Thursday. He made

a flying visit to London to tell me in person it was finished. He's sick of me and doesn't want to see me ever again... Is that plain enough for you?'

'The utter *louse*!' Liz exclaimed, and went on at length at the sleaziness of super-rich playboys.

'My sentiments exactly,' Jemma said and, rising to her feet, added, 'Can we get out of here? I've had enough.'

Jemma had dreaded telling her father, but she discovered she didn't need to. The following weekend she answered a knock on the door, expecting to show a couple around the house, but her father was standing on the doorstep.

'Jemma, are you all right?' To her surprise he put his arms around her and hugged her. 'I'm so sorry. I'd hoped Luke would make you happy, not leave you like this.'

She stepped out of his arms. That Luke had told her father he had left her was the final humiliation. 'Don't worry, Dad, your position in the company and the money from Luke are guaranteed,' she said, with a cynicism that was an instinctive defence against the painful emotions that threatened to engulf her.

'I know—Luke told me. But can't a father worry about his daughter? You must be so upset.'

'No, not really.' She denied her heartache. 'I always knew Luke had the attention span of a gnat when it came to women. Why do you think we broke up in the first place?' Luke wasn't the only one who could embroider the truth about their relationship. 'It was fun while it lasted, but no harm done. Now, really, Dad, much as I'd like you to stay, I have a couple coming to view the house any minute.'

'You're selling the house? I don't blame you. Find something bigger in the luxury class; Luke can certainly afford to pay through the nose for his freedom.'

And on that friendly note her father left. Jemma had to laugh.

But there was very little laughter in the following weeks. She couldn't eat, she couldn't sleep, and it was all Luke Devetzi's fault. She had tried so hard to avoid the pain of loving him, but it had happened anyway.

It was the first day of spring, and Jemma walked out of her doctor's surgery in a state of shock. She had made the appointment because she had fainted at work and Liz had bullied her into it.

It was a miracle—she was pregnant! Elation bubbled up inside her. According to the doctor it was not uncommon to have some spotting in the first weeks of pregnancy—which she'd thought was a light period—and he had calculated she was just over three months pregnant. The timing could not be more perfect, Jemma thought, almost dancing along the street to her car. She had sold her house, and only the previous week moved into a delightful cottage with a large garden in Sussex. If she had harboured any doubts about her decision to move out of London and commute to work three days a week she didn't now. The move had brought her luck already.

'So what did the doctor say?' Liz demanded as Jemma walked into the shop.

'Follow me into the back and I'll tell you.'

'What about Luke?' Liz asked some time later, when Jemma had stopped gushing over the prospect of being a mother. 'You'll have to tell him.'

'No!' Jemma's reaction was immediate, and she hardened her heart against all Liz's arguments to the contrary. 'Oh, come on, Liz. I saw one of your trashy magazines not so long ago, although you tried to hide it, with that picture of Luke with the lovely Davina on his arm. Get real. He was adamant he never wanted to see me again. He sent my belongings from the apartment back to me by courier, for heaven's sake.'

Liz shook her head. 'I didn't know that. What a jerk! But I still think you should tell him; he has a right to know he's going to be a father.'

'If it will make you feel any better, I will if I see him,' Jemma said. *And pigs might fly,* she thought.

A few weeks later Jemma received a letter from Theo. It was to tell her the renovations to the house on Zante were finished, and he hoped the fact she and his grandson had parted would not stop Jemma remaining his friend. She wrote back and told him she had instructed the caretaker to give him a key and allow him to use the house whenever he wished. She felt guilty. But, while she knew she couldn't keep her pregnancy a secret from Luke and Theo for ever, she didn't want them to know just yet. Her emotions were still too raw.

But Jemma got a nasty shock halfway through April, when she and Liz had one of their regular lunches.

'Peter and I were at a business dinner recently, and Luke was there as a special guest. He was alone and he looked terrible. Well, obviously not terrible—he couldn't look terrible if he tried—he's too handsome! But he did look haggard.'

'I'm not surprised with the life he leads,' Jemma said curtly.

'He asked after you…'

Jemma stiffened in her chair. 'Tell me you didn't say anything.'

'No, I simply said you were blooming,' Liz said dryly.

Jemma took maternity leave from the business the next weekend, telling herself it was because she wanted to be super careful of her unborn child. But, if she was honest, it worried her that Liz had met Luke in London. Since their parting she hadn't seen or heard from him, and that was the way she wanted it to stay. The allowance he had made her when they were together was still paid into her bank every month, but she ignored it. At four months her pregnancy was not yet obvious, and no one but Liz knew—which was the way she wanted it for as long as possible.

She loved her cottage, she loved her garden, and she loved the miracle growing inside her. But her love for Luke she locked away in the darkest reaches of her mind. And if sometimes in bed at night it broke free, she made herself a glass of hot milk and thought of her baby. Jemma was a past master at burying her feelings—she had had plenty of practice...

She heard the telephone ring as she looked for her keys in her purse, but by the time Jemma had opened the door and walked into the spacious hall it had stopped. Oh, well, if it was important whoever it was would ring back. She continued to the back of the house and the huge family kitchen-cum-diner. She placed the tin of paint she had bought on the breakfast table and stretched her back. She had finally decided to paint the nursery pale yellow.

She had had a very productive morning—a visit to her new doctor for her six-month pregnancy check, and a trip to the shops to stock up on food for the next week. The house was four miles from the nearest town, tucked away up its own private lane with a copse of trees at one side. It had been built by the previous owner fifty years ago, when he'd married, and he had extended it haphazardly as his family grew until it contained five bedrooms, the master *en-suite*, and three bathrooms. Really it was too big for Jemma, but she had fallen in love with the place. She could sense the love and laughter in the very stones of the house.

Grinning at the thought, Jemma went back out to her car and opened the boot to collect the rest of her shopping. She heard the telephone ring again, and missed it again. Not bothered, Jemma stowed the groceries away and made herself a cup of camomile tea. Picking it up, she walked out of the back door and into the courtyard to look down over the acre of garden. The flowerbeds were a mass of glorious colour among the lush green lawns, and a deep sigh of contentment escaped her.

She settled down on the sunbed beside the fountain in the centre of the courtyard and sipped her tea. The doctor had told her this morning that she was fine. The baby was fine. Life was fine. Draining her cup, she put her feet up, rested her hands lightly on her now protruding stomach and closed her eyes.

Luke recognised Jemma's car, parked his own behind it, and got out. His face flushed with anger, he approached the front door of Wisteria Cottage and pressed the bell. He took a few steps back and looked up at the house. The wisteria was in full bloom, and was trained across the front of the house. A deep blue pantiled roof was inset with four dormer windows, their peaks topped off with wood carvings of flowers. He would have smiled if he hadn't been so furious. It was *so* Jemma's kind of house.

He rang the bell again. She had to be in, but all he could hear was birdsong and the soft sound of insects humming in the hot June air. Impatiently he walked around the side of the house and discovered it was built with two wings. In between them was a courtyard, with a fountain in the centre.

She was pregnant. Even from this distance he could see the swell of her stomach, and rage welled up inside him, gathering the force of a tidal wave.

She was lying on a sunbed, but even as he strode towards her she didn't move. He stopped and stared down at her, his anger laced with anguish. She was so beautiful she took his breath away, and he broke out in a cold sweat, nausea swelling in the pit of his stomach—all the symptoms of the lovesick fool he had hoped he'd put behind him.

She was wearing a soft muslin dress with tiny shoe-string straps; one had slipped off her shoulder, revealing the creamy curve of her breast. One slender arm lay at her side, her other hand rested protectively on the fine fabric covering the pronounced bulge of her stomach. She was carrying his child and she hadn't told him.

'So it's true, Jemma.'

She opened her eyes and thought she was dreaming. 'Luke…' she murmured drowsily. He was wearing chinos and a polo shirt and looked— 'Luke!' she repeated, her eyes finally focusing sharply. This was no dream! Her heart started thudding as he stared back at her, his brows black and jagged above brooding, stormy grey eyes.

'What the hell did you think you were doing, keeping your pregnancy a secret from me?' he demanded harshly.

'I don't know what you mean; my pregnancy is no secret,' Jemma said, rising to her feet, the pain of their parting flooding back, and with it her anger. 'But, as you expressed a desire never to set eyes on me again, it's hardly surprising my condition escaped your notice,' she finished facetiously.

Had she *no* idea what he had gone through the last few months? Sick with longing for her, and unable to sleep, he had worked every hour of the day and night in an attempt to block her from his mind. He'd made a mint of money in the process that he didn't need. But nothing had eased his need for Jemma. In desperation he had taken Davina out—just for dinner—but even that had been a disaster. Now Jemma was standing before him, defiance in her stunning amber eyes, and he had had enough.

'Don't try my patience,' he snarled. 'You know very well what I mean. You never had any intention of telling me you were pregnant. I asked you when we parted if it was a possibility, and you lied and said no. But you're not getting the chance to say no to me again.'

The expression of ferocious anger on his handsome face shocked Jemma to the core. His very presence shocked her. She became intensely aware of his iron-hard body, close to her own, and the scent of him, a mixture of expensive cologne and musky male. She had thought the more advanced stages of pregnancy would diminish her sexual awareness, but it didn't seem to be working!

'I never lied to you. When you mentioned the possibility of me being pregnant, I was bleeding; something I've since learnt is common in the early stages,' she explained—though she didn't owe him an explanation. She didn't owe the swine anything!

She took a step back, and stumbled as her leg hit the seat she had just vacated. With lightning reflexes Luke's arm wrapped around her waist, his hand splayed across the side of her stomach. 'I'm all right,' she snapped, and felt the baby kick against his palm. She saw his features soften and the anger in his eyes turn to awe as they met hers.

'God—the baby kicked. Does it hurt you?' he asked huskily.

'No, I'm fine,' Jemma managed shakily. At least she had been fine before Luke arrived. Now she was anything but! 'You can let me go now, and tell me how you found me and why you're here.'

His arm fell from her waist and he gave her a sardonic glance. 'I'm surprised Liz didn't call to warn you; she seems to be the only person you allow close to you.'

'*Liz* told you? I don't believe you. She wouldn't...' Jemma tailed off as she remembered the two missed telephone calls earlier on.

'Don't worry; Liz didn't betray your trust. Peter did. I met him at a business party last night, and while we were having a whisky together he told me. As a father himself, he thought I deserved to know.'

'Well, now you do.' Jemma managed a nonchalant shrug, but inside she was trembling. After nearly five months she had almost convinced herself that she didn't love Luke, and she certainly didn't need him. She had her new home and her baby to look forward to. But now that she had seen him again her carefully erected defences were in danger of being torn down. Already her nerves were on edge, and she was intensely conscious of him. He was leaner, the frown lines between his black, arched brows deeper, but his sexual magnetism was as potent as ever.

'What do you want, Luke?' she asked carefully. She was legally still his wife, and he could make it very difficult for her if he chose to exercise his paternal rights over the child. He could destroy her tentatively constructed new life, and make any thought of rearing her baby on her own look very dodgy. At the very least he could insist on regular access to the child. 'And can you hurry up? I've already been in the sun long enough for one day.'

'You're my wife and you are carrying my child,' Luke

said with icy precision, and he scooped her up in his arms before she could even guess his intention.

'Are you crazy? Put me down!' Jemma screeched furiously, but had to grasp his neck for support as he strode purposefully towards the house.

'No. What I want is to protect you and my child, and you're right—you have had too much sun,' he told her as he shouldered through the door into the spacious kitchen. He slowly lowered her to her feet, his silver eyes flicking curiously around the room. 'This is nice.'

'I'm not interested in your opinion,' Jemma shot back furiously. 'And I don't know what your game is, but I can tell you now you're wasting your time. I don't want you here.' Turning her back on him, she walked towards the sink, needing a glass of water to cool down.

Luke caught her shoulder and spun her around, his determined silver eyes locking onto hers. 'You have no choice.' Where had she heard that before? she wondered with bitter resentment. Nothing had changed. 'I'm staying here for as long as it takes. For ever if I have to. I love you, and I'm damned if I'll let you go again.'

Jemma stared up at him, amazed. She couldn't have heard him right. 'Say that again.'

He ran a distracted hand through his black hair. 'I love you, Jemma. I always have,' he said, his deep voice thick with emotion.

She heard the words and for a moment she almost believed him—until she felt her baby move inside her. 'No,' she said. 'No, I don't believe you.' How could she have forgotten even for an instant that Luke was a master manipulator who quite ruthlessly used his fierce intelligence and considerable power to get what he wanted? And he wanted her baby. 'You're lying just to get my baby.' And with the realisation came an equally abhorrent thought:

Luke must have somehow discerned she loved him, and now he was offering her what he thought she wanted…

'I have no reason to lie, Jemma. I'm the father of your child, and the baby is mine whatever happens between us. But it's you I love,' he insisted. Reaching for her, he eased her right up against the length of his body and added, 'It's you I need in my life—desperately. I've tried living without you and it was a living hell.'

There was harshness in his voice that touched her heart. She looked up into his eyes and saw deep emotion in the silver depths. She began to weaken. Dear heaven, she wanted him to love her so much… 'You have to believe me, because I can't let you go again.'

His comment was like a douche of cold water; she'd been in danger of believing him—but no more. Suddenly all the emotion and resentment she had suppressed for months came bubbling to the surface. She placed her hands on his chest and forced some space between them.

'You never *let me go*, Luke. As I recall, you walked out on me, declaring you never wanted to see me again—and I know why!' she spat. 'What kind of an idiot do you take me for? You come into my home, declare undying love for me, and expect me to fall at your feet. Well, I've got news for you. I can see through your little game with my eyes closed,' she raged. 'Do you think I don't know about Davina? I know you were dating her before you married me—the Davina who was with you when I called you on your birthday and you passed off as your PA. The very same Davina I saw you photographed with in a magazine recently.'

His hands fell from her and he stepped back, dark colour staining his high cheekbones.

'Don't bother denying it,' she jeered. 'I suppose the pair of you thought it was some sophisticated joke to pretend to be talking to me on the phone when she was the object of your sexy conversation. You know what? You make me sick. And as for your supposedly caring suggestion that I look for a house because you knew the apartment didn't suit me, why didn't you just tell me you wanted me to leave then? But, no, that was too simple for your Machiavellian mind. And to think I had actually decided to put the past behind me and make our marriage work. That sure as hell was one of life's little ironies.' She shook her head and laughed a bitter, humourless laugh. 'Oh, just get lost, Luke. I'm going to rest.' And with that she turned to walk out of the kitchen, shaking with the force of her emotional outburst.

'Oh, no, you don't, Jemma,' Luke said, pulling her back in his arms. 'You're not running away now. You were actually jealous of Davina,' he stated, his eyes now gleaming silver with relief. 'Have you any idea how happy that makes me feel? Knowing that you've felt even a fraction of the jealousy that has gnawed at my soul since I met you?' Jemma opened her mouth to deny it, but he didn't give her the chance. 'Have you any idea how long I've waited to break through your super-cool control? How much I've longed to reach you on a deeper level? How often I lay in bed beside you sated with sex but knowing that you were keeping a wall between us, your deeper emotions locked away with your dead husband? You can't begin to know what it did to me. Me—Luke Devetzi—who never believed in love.' He gave her a look of wry self-mockery. 'And I fell hopelessly in love with a woman who was locked in the memory of her past love.'

Jemma looked into his eyes, saw the vulnerability in the shimmering depths and caught her breath. This was a Luke she had never seen before, and she watched him with an aching uncertainty and a wary hope—because she wanted to believe him but was afraid of getting hurt again. 'So when did this momentous realisation come to you?' she asked, using sarcasm to protect her inner feelings.

He smiled down into her eyes. 'I realised on the day we visited the house on Zante, lying on the bed in your aunt's bedroom, that I loved you,' he said huskily, and Jemma could scarcely breathe. 'Later on the beach I had to listen to you quite calmly say that I didn't believe in love, and I wanted to tell you then but I knew it was too soon.' His arms tightened around her and he looked deep into her eyes. 'You lied to me when you told me you didn't know your aunt's lover, and that hurt because it proved you didn't trust me.'

Jemma stiffened. 'You're guessing now,' she muttered, very flushed, and he smiled at her with knowing eyes.

'I've studied you minutely, but forget it; you don't need to tell me. I vowed then I would do everything in my power to earn your trust and hopefully your love.'

Jemma dared not believe it. Luke was such a smooth operator, so plausible and convincing, and yet held in his arms she almost did believe him. 'You said there was no such thing as love, that it was only another word for lust.' She looked frowningly up at him. 'You also said you were sick of me, so why should I believe your apparent change of heart now?' she asked.

'I said a damn sight too much,' Luke muttered, his mouth twisting. 'How can I make you understand? Any dumb idea I ever had about love went out of the window the moment I set eyes on you. You were the woman of my dreams, but it turned into a nightmare when you said you were married. I spent a year trying to forget you—a celibate year. Finally, in desperation, I dated Davina—and then I met you again and I swear I've never touched Davina since. She paid a surprise visit to my office to wish me a happy birthday, but I made her leave before I spoke to you. Do you think I could speak like that, make love with another woman the way I do with you?' he demanded harshly. 'You are my love, my passion, my life.'

She remembered the passion, the gentleness, the myriad ways he had made love to her, and her heart squeezed in her breast. Was he telling the truth?

'When I forced you to marry me I told myself it didn't matter that you were still in love with Alan. I wanted you, I knew we were very sexually compatible, and I thought we could base a marriage on that. But I very quickly realised I was wrong. I loved you, and I wanted much, much more from you.' He put a hand under her chin and tilted her head right back. 'Look at me, Jemma,' he commanded, and she looked into his blazing silver eyes and wondered how she had ever thought they were cold. Because they were burning right now, with a need and a pain that made her heart stutter.

'I am a very possessive man, and it shames me to say it, but I was insanely jealous of your dead husband.'

'You broke my locket deliberately,' Jemma murmured.

'If he had been alive I would have broken his neck. That's how despicable I am,' he responded immediately.

Jemma's eyes widened to their fullest extent. Luke's face was haggard and drawn, as if he was suffering some mental torture. 'You don't mean that, Luke.'

'Maybe not. But when I dashed back from New York that last time I was determined to tell you how I truly felt, because after our intimate conversation I was convinced that I was finally getting somewhere with you—especially as you'd agreed to look for a house.'

'I thought you meant for *us*, but then afterwards I

thought it was your way of telling me to leave,' Jemma interjected.

'You were right the first time.' Luke attempted a smile. 'But when I found you in tears in your old home something snapped inside me.' He closed his eyes for a moment in remembered anguish, then opened them again. 'God! Jemma, can you ever forgive me? I very nearly took you without your consent.'

'*No!*' Jemma cried. She couldn't bear to see the torment in his eyes. 'You didn't. You were angry at first, but I was with you all the way,' she said, blushing furiously, the hope in her heart growing by the minute.

'Thank you for that. But I realised then that I couldn't trust myself around you, that I had to leave.'

'But you said you were sick of me. I saw the disgust in your eyes,' Jemma couldn't help reminding him.

'I was disgusted at myself. I was never sick of you. I quoted Proverbs—"Hope deferred maketh the heart sick"—and that was how I felt. The sex was wonderful, but I was getting more and more desperate—hoping that you'd come to love me. I'm a selfish man and I wanted all of you. Body and soul. I wanted to be the centre of your universe. I'd tried everything I could to make you love me, and nothing had worked. My hopes were in shreds and I had to leave before I destroyed what little feeling you had left for me.' His hand fell from her chin. 'I'm not surprised you never told me you were pregnant; you're probably afraid of me.'

Jemma could not bear to hear her proud, indomitable Luke sounding so humble. 'Afraid of you, Luke…never,' she said with a smile. If she wanted him she had to let go of her fears and trust that he was telling her the truth.

'I hope you mean that, Jemma,' he said fiercely. 'Because I'm going to be around you and our baby for a very, very long time.'

He hadn't stayed humble for long, Jemma thought, smiling to herself. Sliding her hands up over his chest, she linked her fingers around his neck. Swaying into him as far as her bump would allow, she pulled his proud head down to hers, her pulse racing at her own audacity. 'That's fine by me,' she breathed. 'I like the idea of the man I love being around me and our child.' She saw the shock in his eyes, and then his mouth closed over hers in a hungry open-mouthed kiss that was incredibly tender, yet erotic.

'Tell me,' Luke pleaded, lifting his dark head, one hand winding through the soft strands of hair that tumbled down her back, the other hand curving around her nape. 'Tell me this is for real.' His cheekbones were flushed and his silver eyes gleamed with a feverish light. 'Tell me again you love me.'

She pulled back a little. 'I love you, Luke.' Her full lips parted in a beaming smile and her pulse raced even faster as she heard his groan of satisfaction. He kissed her with a deep, urgent desire that touched her soul. His hand moved from her nape to stroke over her breasts, and then down over the hard mound of her stomach.

'I shouldn't be doing this.' He groaned again. 'You're pregnant.'

'Yes, you should,' Jemma said, her breasts swelling beneath the soft fabric of her dress, warmth coursing through her veins and exciting every nerve in her body. 'But not here—upstairs,' she murmured, and he lifted her tenderly in his arms and carried her where she said. Then he slid her gently to her feet and stepped back a pace. He looked at her in silence for what seemed an age, his eyes darkening until they resembled the deepest slate, and suddenly Jemma was nervous.

'Do you like my bedroom?' she asked.

'You fill my eyes. You fill my heart. You fill my mind to the exclusion of all else.' He reached for her shoulders and his hands shook as his fingers caught the slender straps and eased them down her arms, the white muslin pooling at her feet. 'My God!' he exclaimed huskily, his gaze roaming over her altered figure. 'I thought you were perfect before—but now, ripe with my child, you are…' He swallowed hard, his eyes filling with moisture. 'You are exquisite beyond belief.'

'Luke…' she prompted hesitantly. She had never seen him so distressed.

'You are heartbreakingly beautiful,' he said, and moved a hand to the back of her head, holding her close against his shoulder, stroking her long hair, his face hidden from her view. 'I don't deserve you, Jemma, but I love you madly and I always will.' She felt his chest heave and tilted her head back, her golden gaze meshing with his. All her doubts and fears vanished at the love and need that blazed from his silver eyes.

'Luke,' she said again, trembling, and his mouth moved hotly over her brow, her cheek and finally down to claim her lips. He lifted her and laid her on the bed as gently as if she was made of glass, and, shrugging out of his clothes, lay down beside her.

His fingers stroked her breast, and a soft cry of pleasure broke from her. His head bent and his mouth took hers again, while his hands moved gently and unhurriedly over her naked flesh. Jemma reached for him, her hands shaping his shoulders and down the strong line of his back as passion flared deep inside her.

'Jemma, my darling,' he murmured against her flesh as

he caressed her with growing urgency. Her nails dug suddenly into his back and she heard his guttural groan as he finally possessed her.

It was like nothing that had gone before—a true melding of body and mind, the rhythm of love gentle, growing in ever-building waves of passion to explode in a climax of absolute unity where all sense of self was lost in the wonder and glory of being one.

Afterwards Luke held her in the curve of his shoulder, kissing her hair, his hand slowly stroking over her stomach, and said teasingly, 'Well, at least Theo will be pleased; his great-grandchild will get his old house.'

'What?' She glanced up at him and saw the laughter in his luminous eyes. 'You mean you weren't pleased?'

'"Pleased" doesn't begin to describe the depths of my love for you. I love you more than I can say, Jemma.'

'Then show me again.' She grinned, and he did.

EPILOGUE

IT WAS September, with the sun blazing out of a clear blue sky and the sound of childish laughter echoing in the heavy air. Jemma leant over the balcony of their bedroom, smiling to herself as she watched Theo, Milo and her son Alex splashing about in the pool below.

All those months ago, alone and pregnant, she could never have imagined such happiness.

'Jemma, it's after nine. Maria's packed an overnight bag for you; all you have to do is get ready.' Luke came up behind her and slipped an arm around her waist. 'This is our second wedding anniversary, remember, and we have to get going.'

She cast him a droll look. 'You've reminded me it's our wedding anniversary at least three times since midnight.'

Luke smiled down at her, a reminiscent gleam in his silver eyes. 'Yes, and I will again—I promise,' he chuckled. 'But not right now; the helicopter's on its way and I want to get there before nightfall. I have a surprise for you.'

'Are you sure Alex will be okay on his own?'

'On his own!' Luke arched an eyebrow at her. 'You are joking; with a staff of six who dote on him, and Theo and Milo totally besotted with him, our son will not have a second to call his own.'

'Yes, you're right,' she said, turning in his arms and planting a swift kiss on his chin. 'I'll go and shower.' She saw the flash of interest in his grey gaze. 'On my own.'

182

She laughed and spun out of his arms. 'We're in a hurry, remember?'

Jemma was still smiling when she turned on the shower. The last fourteen months had been sheer bliss. They divided their time between this fabulous house outside Athens and Wisteria Cottage in England, with occasional visits to the holiday home on Zante. Their son Alex had been born at Wisteria Cottage with the help of a farmer's wife—much to Luke's dismay. He had arranged for a top London hospital, but baby Alex had not wanted to wait. He'd come into the world the day before their first wedding anniversary, the image of his father, with a mass of black hair, crying lustily.

Turning off the shower, Jemma dried herself and dressed casually, as Luke had instructed, in white cotton trousers and a navy and white Donna Karan shirt. Yesterday the house had been full of friends and neighbours with their children, for Alex's first birthday party, and amid all the excitement he had actually taken his first few steps.

'Damn it, Jemma, come on—the helicopter is waiting.' Luke appeared at the bedroom door, wearing tailored Bermuda shorts and a polo shirt. He looked gorgeous and vibrant and Jemma couldn't have wished for a more devoted and sexy husband. Even if he did get a bit impatient at times.

An hour later, after a protracted goodbye to Alex, they headed for the helicopter parked in the grounds. Luke was muttering darkly, 'We're only going away for one night, for heaven's sake.' Jemma smiled to herself; he had spent as much time hugging and kissing Alex goodbye as she had.

Jemma was surprised when the helicopter landed and they stepped out onto the roof of the hotel on Zante where they had spent their wedding night. She glanced quizzically up at Luke as he took her hand in his and led her down into the hotel. It was a nice thought, but not a very original surprise. They dined here frequently when they stayed at the house in the bay.

'I know what you're thinking.' Luke looped an arm around her shoulders and held her close. 'But this is not the surprise—simply the safest and nearest place to land.'

'So where are we going?'

'Patience, woman.'

But her patience was wearing very thin after a short car ride which deposited them at the steps that led down to their very own holiday home.

Luke stopped at the base of the steps and grinned, his grey eyes gleaming with wicked humour. 'Now we come to the good part; I get to blindfold you.'

He looked gorgeous with the sun gleaming on his black hair, his handsome face relaxed in a smile. 'This wouldn't have anything to do with kinky sex, would it?' Jemma asked.

'Shame on you,' Luke mocked. 'The very opposite, in fact.' Jemma made a small moue of disappointment as he tied a black scarf around her eyes and, with a guiding hand around her waist, led her forward. She felt the paving beneath her feet, and then soil, before he stopped.

'This is it,' he announced, and removed the blindfold from her eyes. 'I hope you like it.'

She was standing by the rockery she had built for her aunt, and, looking up, she gasped. Six feet up, cut into the cliff face, was an oval niche lined with blue mosaic tiles and containing a perfectly sculptured statue of the Madonna and child. Tears flooded her eyes, and unashamedly she let them fall.

Luke's arms wrapped around her. 'I know you said your aunt Mary would have liked a gravestone but she didn't think it was right somehow. I thought you might like this instead.' His hand rubbed up and down her back. 'I'm sorry if I was wrong. Please don't cry. I can't bear to see you cry,' Luke groaned against her hair.

Jemma tilted back her head, a tremulous smile on her lips, her eyes swimming with tears of joy tinged with sadness for what the statue represented. She knew Luke loved her, he had shown her in a thousand ways, but that her formidable husband had had the sensitivity to think of such a marvellous present overwhelmed her. 'You weren't wrong, Luke. I love it—and I love you,' she said, her heart in her eyes. 'I would never have thought of it, but I'm sure Aunt Mary would have approved; it's the most wonderful surprise ever.'

'It's a Greek thing, I suppose,' Luke husked, and brushed his lips against hers, then slipped his tongue into the sweet moistness with an ever-deepening pleasure. Finally, when he lifted his head to let her breathe, he added, 'I must confess I do have another motive for bringing you here.'

'You do?' Enfolded in the warmth of his embrace, his aroused state very evident against her belly, her pulse racing and her heart overflowing with love, she had a good idea what he had in mind.

She wasn't exactly wrong…

'Yes, it's a family tradition I want to revive,' he said, nuzzling her neck where the pulse beat heavily in her throat, his hand stroking over her breast. 'Theo was conceived on this beach, and so was my mother. With your agreement, I want our next child to share the tradition.'

Nine months later, Lucy Marie did…

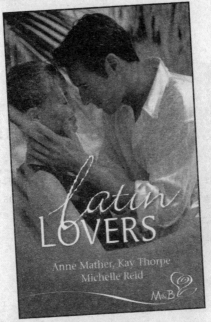

4 FREE

BOOKS AND A SURPRISE GIFT!

We would like to take this opportunity to thank you for reading this Mills & Boon® book by offering you the chance to take FOUR more specially selected titles from the Modern Romance™ series absolutely FREE! We're also making this offer to introduce you to the benefits of the Reader Service™—

- ★ FREE home delivery
- ★ FREE gifts and competitions
- ★ FREE monthly Newsletter
- ★ Exclusive Reader Service offers
- ★ Books available before they're in the shops

Accepting these FREE books and gift places you under no obligation to buy, you may cancel at any time, even after receiving your free shipment. Simply complete your details below and return the entire page to the address below. You don't even need a stamp!

YES! Please send me 4 free Modern Romance books and a surprise gift. I understand that unless you hear from me, I will receive 6 superb new titles every month for just £2.75 each, postage and packing free. I am under no obligation to purchase any books and may cancel my subscription at any time. The free books and gift will be mine to keep in any case.

P6ZED

Ms/Mrs/Miss/Mr ....Initials ....
BLOCK CAPITALS PLEASE

Surname ....

Address ....

....

....Postcode.............................

Send this whole page to:
UK: FREEPOST CN81, Croydon, CR9 3WZ.